DARK REDEMPTION

THE DARK CREATURES SAGA - BOOK 4

ELLA STONE

ALSO BY ELLA STONE

Dark Creatures Prequel Novellas
Mother of Wolves

Son of a Vampire

Man and Wolf

Call of the Grimoire

The Dark Creatures Saga
Dark Creatures

Dark Destiny

Dark Deception

Dark Redemption

Dark Reckoning

The Bloodsuckers Blog Series
Life Sucks

Love Bites

Lost Souls

This story is a work of fiction. All names, characters, organisations, places, events and incidents are products of the author's imagination or are used fictitiously. Any resemblance to any persons, alive or dead, events or locals is entirely coincidental.

Text copyright © 2021 Ella Stone

Second edition published 2024

Paper Cat Publishing

ISBN: 979-8780552376

Edited by Carol Worwood

All rights reserved.

No part of this book should be reproduced in any way without the express permission of the author.

1

Narissa

The picture on the monitor shows a single bed and a person sitting on it. This is what it's come to. Me, watching my best friend via CCTV, unable to get any closer to her for fear of what she might do. She knows I'm here. She knows I'm watching her. Her gaze is locked onto the ceiling-mounted camera and she's staring straight at me. A cold shiver runs down my spine. She looks so similar to the Rey I used to know, until you look into those eyes.

"I brought you some nectarines."

Oliver's voice comes through the speaker.

"I saw them this morning and remembered how much you like them. We used to buy them at the farmers' market in Camden, remember?"

Her blank expression turns into a sneer.

"Wow. Let me guess. You're hoping that maybe I'll bite into the sweet, juicy flesh and all those old memories of how perfect my life used to be will flood in, and then I'll be magically transformed into the kind, loving girl I was before."

Oliver remains as unruffled as always.

"No, I just thought you might like some nectarines, that's all. Although, and this might surprise you, we are actually trying to help you here."

This time her sneer is accompanied by a laugh, so malevolent it seems to drain all the warmth from the air around me.

"You still don't get it, do you?" she spits at him. "I don't need help. This is me. This is who I am meant to be. This is the most free and happy I have ever been in my life. Or at least I would be, if you took these off me."

She lifts her hands, indicating the manacles around her wrists, the thick metal cuffs linked by a rusty chain. I dread to think what they were originally used for, but right now, they're one of the ways we're managing to keep Rey's magic under control. These measures include: repeat doses of vampire sedative, administered by Calin's nail; not letting anything made of glass come remotely within her reach; and stopping her having access to daylight, too, which is harsh but necessary. When we first brought her here, we placed her in one of the many guest bedrooms. It was fairly compact and had a small window, just enough to catch a glimpse of the outside world and let in a little sunlight. Just enough, it turned out, for her to cause a violent thunderstorm. The rain hammered down like bullets and made it impossible for anyone to go outside. We learned, though. She's now in a disused coal store, a windowless, bare, brick lean-to at the back of the house, with an LED Perspex bulb as the only illumination. (We removed the glass one for obvious reasons.) Even the lens of the camera that's relaying the pictures to me is made of plastic. It's just what we have to do.

It's been three months now. I sometimes almost manage to convince myself that she's improving, that she's a little different, speaking to us a little more civilly, that it's taking a little longer before she reacts and tries again to extract herself from the shackles. But I know it's just wishful thinking. She's not getting worse, though. I suppose that's something. But she's not getting better. Not by a long shot.

Oliver drags a chair into view and sits down in front of her, far closer than I'd dare, but he's braver when it comes to dealing with her. I hate myself for thinking about her like this, as if she's some rabid animal, but frankly, that's how she's behaving. Aggressive. Unpredictable. Terrifying.

"The thing is," he says, looking directly at her, "you seem to forget. I knew you before. The real you. And I know you're still in there."

She offers a short, bitter chuckle. He carries on, regardless.

"You're making a good job of keeping this up, but the Rey I know is strong. Whatever dark magic the vampires forced you to perform, whatever hold they had on you, I know that, sooner or later, the real Rey, the one we love, is going to shake it off. And when you do, we'll be waiting for you."

There's no laughter now. Just the dark gleam of narrowed eyes as she glowers at him. I know exactly what's angered her. He did it on purpose, just to see how she'd react.

"*We?*"

Her lips curl in a sneer as she speaks.

"Why on earth would you encumber yourself with her like that? You know she doesn't care about anyone but herself."

He cocks his head, as if showing moderate interest.

"Am I supposed to know who you're talking about?"

"You know exactly who I'm taking about it. If you want someone to blame for the way I am, then you need look no further than her."

"The way you are? A moment ago, you told me you were the best you'd ever been."

Her sneer deepens into a snarl, like an animal caught in a trap. Though, this time, it was her own words that ensnared her.

"Tell me, why won't you speak to Naz? Is it because you're afraid?"

"Afraid!" she snorts. "Of what?"

"Oh, I don't know. Maybe the humanity you might start to feel. Or perhaps the memories you'd be forced to recall."

A sly smile crosses her face.

"You and I made plenty of those, didn't we? And much more fun ones, too. Remember that time in the park, under that willow tree? That was real eye-opener. Why don't you unlock these cuffs and I'll show you a few new tricks I've learnt on my travels?"

"Really? You think I'd fall for that?"

She kicks out at him, but he blocks her with his hand, and she's immediately back to twisting and writhing on the bed, trying to get out of her chains.

"I know you're there, Narissa!" she yells, with her eyes locked on the camera again. "I know you're watching this! I know you're watching me! I'm going to make you pay for what you did to me! I'm going to make you pay for everything!"

Standing up, I switch off the speaker, but her words resonate through my brain, and I can tell from the image that she's still screaming at me, staring up at the camera with those hollow, black eyes.

I turn away and grab a glass of water from the table. The door creaks open behind me.

"How's it going?" Calin asks, quietly slipping into the room, which is one of the smallest in this vast building. Under normal circumstances, it would be plenty big enough for two people. But these are not normal circumstances and being in the same place—of any size—as Calin, is more than I can deal with right now. My first instinct is to leave, to not even speak to him, but there are things I need to say.

"Oliver is making no progress at all. But you knew that would be the case. You need to let me have another go and talking to her."

"That's not a good idea."

"I don't agree."

"Last time, she performed a choking spell on you. And the time before that she managed to set your clothes on fire. You just being near her seems to somehow amplify her powers, and you know it."

"That was over a month ago. Things could be different now."

"Yes, exactly. They could be even worse."

I know he's not going to give in, and I hate him even more. Hate him? Hate? Is that the right word for what I feel? In some ways, yes, it very much is.

As I turn to leave, he grabs my hand.

"Narissa, please. I've given you space, just as you asked. I've given you weeks and weeks of space, but this is becoming ridiculous. Can we please talk? Can we just sit down together and have a conversation?"

He's pleading with his eyes. There's so much hurt there. And I'm glad. He deserves it.

"There's nothing for us to talk about."

"Please, Narissa."

I yank my hand free and snarl in a way that reminds me too much of this new Rey for comfort.

"I don't have time for this. I need to go for a run."

"But—"

"Goodbye, Calin."

I manoeuvre past him, trying not to let any part of my body touch his and make for the door. I want to get as far away from him as possible.

2

Given the dimness of the observation room, I'd forgotten that it was the middle of the day. Light streams through the corridor windows in wide shafts, illuminating the dust motes that dance around the thick, velvety curtains. Of all the places I have ever stayed, this one has the most magnificent drapes but also the most dust. It's not really surprising, though, with a house this size. It must be an almost impossible task to keep everything clean, and the owner is hardly up to climbing ladders to brush the coving. It's actually more of a chateau than a house, nestling on the edge of a huge national park, near the French town of Alès.

I head across a large hallway with varnished, wooden floors. I'm about to open the front door, when a singsong voice with a French lilt to it calls to me from outside the kitchen.

"Narissa, ma chérie, I thought that was you. Come

dear, come. Henri has made some pastries. They're just out of the oven. I thought you might like a little refreshment."

"That's very kind, Régine, but I was actually just about to go for a run."

"Then you should have something to keep your energy up before you go. And you can assist me carrying them to the drawing room so everyone can help themselves. Tell the others when you go outside. Come, come my sweet, you can spare a minute or two for an old lady, can't you?"

There's a twinkle in her eye that tells me she knows I won't refuse her. Of course, I wouldn't. She's our hostess and we are guests in her home. And it's not an understatement to say that we've landed on our feet here.

For the first part of my time on the run, Oliver and I were living off whatever he could catch: fish, birds, rabbits. When we managed to earn some money from prize fighting, we were able to buy food, but honestly, in the three months that we've been staying with Régine, it feels like I've eaten more than in the last three years combined.

Following her into the kitchen, I pick up one of the trays of pastries. She wasn't exaggerating. They're still warm and they're simply oozing with goats' cheese. Their aroma is so inviting, I'm tempted to tuck straight in. But I carry them out across the hallway and into the drawing room. Drawing room, dining room, sunroom, snug, library, anti-library—honestly, this place has more names for rooms than I would have thought possible, although to be fair, with the number of us staying here right now, they're all needed.

"Thank you, ma chérie. I am very grateful. These old

arms aren't quite what they were. Now sit, sit." She waves her hands. "Enjoy one, before the rabble arrives and devours them all."

I know that attempting to refuse her would be an utter waste of time, so I give in without any further objections and grab one from the top—a thin pastry covered in pieces of crushed pistachio.

"And I've asked Henri to prepare pheasant for dinner again tonight. Those young wolf men enjoyed it so much last week, I thought we'd have it again. I suggested he cooks a little extra this time. Your kind certainly have an appetite, don't they?"

Catching the crumbs in my hand, I finish my mouthful before speaking.

"Régine, you don't have to go to all this trouble. The wolves can find food for themselves and if not, we'd be fine making ourselves toast or sandwiches."

"Toast, as a main meal, in this house? Zut alors. Don't be ridiculous. Besides, it's been such a long time since I've had guests. How long, I dread to think. Please, allow me the privilege of spoiling you. You will probably be the last I get to do this for. You know, there was a time when the house was often so full, you could barely move for people. And all the dancing and the music. Oh, là là! It was merveilleux. Those parties … they were something else."

I was told this story when we arrived. We were a sorry sight that first night, with Oliver bloody from vampire bites and Rey drugged and bruised from fighting her handcuffs and twenty wolves. These latter were in human form but dressed in an odd variety of clothing that they had acquired on the journey over here.

I didn't know what to expect. Calin lead us down a vast gravel driveway lined with cypress trees and lifted the metal knocker on the ornate front door. An old friend that we could trust, was all he'd told us, and so I'd assumed it would be another vampire. A rich, old vampire. Instead, the door was opened by an elderly man in a butler's uniform, and moments later, this frail old woman, dressed in a lavish, silk dress, appeared in front of us. Her eyes lit up at the sight of Calin, her smile broad as she embraced him, clutching him tightly, before turning her attention to the rest of us and beckoning us all inside.

"Come in. Come in. Come in."

She didn't ask questions as we stumbled over the threshold, Oliver held upright by two pairs of strong hands. I still haven't discussed with her where we came from or why we need to stay here, but I expect Calin has filled her in on all the details. Their evening walks together are very much a ritual.

"The first time I met your friend, Calin, was at one of those parties," Régine says, lowering herself slowly into a comfortable, wingback chair and motions for me to take another. I can tell by the way her voice has become reflective that she's going to tell me the story once again. Given how much she does for us, I consider it fair payment to listen to it each time, as if it were the first. Knowing this could take a while, I pick up another couple of pastries and settle in for the familiar tale.

"Oh, my parents loved parties," she says, her eyes lost

in the past. "If they'd had their way, they would have held one every night. It sometimes felt like they did, when I was a child. Always different people in our home. Every time new guests. You know, I think it may have been because they preferred talking to others than to each other. Or to me. But *c'est la vie*. I would sneak out and sit at the top of the stairs and watch as they arrived, the women in their beautiful dresses and the men so handsome. The adults would carry on as if I were not there. Until him, that is. He was the only one who ever really saw me.

"I was so young, maybe six or seven, the first time he visited. It was another party, of course, but there was something different about this one. My parents were entertaining *special guests*, and I was not to leave my bedroom. *Interdit.* That was the word they used. Forbidden. But you cannot stop children from doing their own thing, particularly if you have no intention of minding them properly.

"That night, I was in my usual place, listening to the music, when I heard another noise. Not conversation or laughter. It sounded like muffled screaming, coming from one of the bedrooms. I thought that perhaps someone had got locked in or needed help. Then again, maybe I thought none of those things. Maybe I was just being nosey. It's difficult to remember after such a long time. Anyway, as I followed the sound to where it was coming from, it got louder, more recognisable. It was a man. A man in great pain, I was certain. As I reached to open the door, Calin swept me up in his arms. And he was beautiful. As beautiful then as he is today. He took me back to the top of the stairs and said, in flawless French, *"I'm sure it is far too late for you to be up."*

"I can stay up to whatever time I wish," I told him.

"Is that right"?

"It is."

"And I suppose you can eat whatever you like, too. Because I believe I spotted some delicious-looking ice cream in the parlour."

"He was so charmant. So sweet. And he knew just how to distract a young child. And then, in the kitchen, away from the other adults, he listened to me talk, rabbiting on about silly childish things as I ate my bowl of ice cream. By the time he took me back up to my bedroom, I'd completely forgotten about the screaming. I didn't think about it until days later.

"After this, whenever my parents had *that sort of party*, he would fetch me downstairs and talk with me as I ate ice cream, or sorbet, or some little treat that he had brought me from his travels. As I grew older, the conversations continued. I told him about school, about boys too, although I think he knew I always had a soft spot for him. But he never took advantage of that. Never used me, not for my blood nor for anything else. Sometimes, when I think back to those nights, I wonder who it was escaping from reality—me or him?"

She looks up at me with a wistful smile.

"And now, I am grateful that I can be of some assistance to him, to all of you."

"You're helping us enormously, just by letting us stay here, Régine. You don't need to let us eat you out of house

CHAPTER 2

and home, too. And really, pheasant seems a little extravagant."

"Did someone say pheasant?"

Lou is standing in the doorway. It's hard to believe it's less than a year since I first met this girl, who I now consider more of a sister than a friend. She's matured a lot in that time, we both have, but I blame myself for some of the changes that have been forced on her. Yet she never seems fazed. She's never anything less than perfectly optimistic.

"That recipe Henri used last time was incredible. Is he going to do it the same way, with the roast potatoes, too? If he is, please don't tell the boys. They ate almost all of it before the rest of us had a chance. Maybe we should have different mealtimes, just to make sure that everyone gets their fair share. Although, in that case, Mum should eat with the boys. You know what she's like when it comes to his food."

It's special watching Régine's face light up when Lou goes into one of her massive rambles, and I get it completely. Even when your best friend is chained up in a dark room, her body taken over by dark magic, and the vampire you had possible feelings for but definite sex with hides your mother's death from you, Lou can still somehow make you smile. It's a talent, that's for sure.

"Do not worry, Loulou. I will make sure to tell him to do extra just for you."

"You're amazing, Régine," she says and comes and kisses her on both cheeks, then notices something.

"Are those fresh pastries?" she asks, moving over to grab one.

"Did you want something, Lou," I say, as I watch her shovel one, then another of the amazing French delicacies into her mouth. "Or did you just come here to drop crumbs all over the rug?"

"Oops, sorry. I'll clear that up," she replies, looking down at the mess she's made. "I was just looking for you, that's all."

"Why's that?"

"I was wondering if you were thinking of going for a run."

A run. Yes, that's absolutely what I'd planned on doing before I sat down with Régine and started eating.

"I'm just going to finish this, first," I say, indicating the food in my own hand.

"Cool, great," she says, her feet shifting slightly on the floor. "That'd be great. Brill."

"Lou … what is it?"

"Nothing," she replies, her eyes now shifting almost as much as her feet. "Nothing at all. Only …"

"Only what?"

Her face contorts into a grimace which looks part painful, part guilty.

"You should probably be prepared. That's all."

3

I wish I didn't know what she was referring to, but I do. It's been the same for weeks now. Just when it seems everything is going okay—or as okay as it can be—the wolves bring it up again. They're tenacious. I'll give them that.

"Maybe I'll go for a run later," I say, bending down and kissing Régine goodbye.

"Don't be late for dinner," she calls, as I leave the room with Lou on my heels. In a house this size, it would be easy to shake her, but I'm better than that. The moment I pause to decide which way to go, I can feel her breathing down my neck.

"Just come and listen to what they have to say."

"Why? I already know what it will be, and you already know how I'd reply."

"But things have changed since we last spoke about it. The last mission went brilliantly. Best yet, by a long way.

Everyone agrees. And you were amazing. You are always amazing."

"The last mission was three days long."

"Exactly."

"Three days is not a lifetime, Lou."

Upstairs seems like my best option. I managed to score my own bedroom in the chateau, and so far, everyone has respected my privacy there, even with Lou and Chrissie in the next room. However, today it seems my luck may have run out. As I turn onto the staircase, Lou somehow jumps across the banister and lands in front of me, blocking my path.

"Please Naz," she says, offering me her best puppy-dog eyes. "I told them that I'd get you to listen. They're expecting you. Just do it for me, please? Five minutes. That's all. Five minutes and I promise you won't get pestered for another week."

"Another month."

"How about until after the next mission?" she tries, but my glare says it all. "Fine then. A month. No one will say anything more about it for four weeks. Assuming you don't agree, that is."

I let out a heavy, reluctant sigh. If it's not one thing, it's another. I guess I'd better get this over and done with as soon as possible. I turn around and head back across the hallway—which is bigger than my entire first flat, by the way—and out of the front door.

I suspect that, once, these gardens were incredible. Even now, with their overgrown rose bushes and unpruned hedgerows, they're still an impressive sight. It's November, and the landscape is awash with ambers and oranges. The lavender bushes have gone to seed, but the aroma as I pass them is simply divine. Not that there's much time to dwell on that—within moments of stepping outside, I'm accosted by twenty-one massive wolves.

Every single pair of yellow eyes is on me. Not long ago, I would have found this intimidating, if not terrifying. But those days are long gone.

"Maybe it would be easier if you change into the wolf?" Lou says hopefully.

"Nope. They want this conversation, then they can have it as humans."

I place my hands on my hips, making my intentions quite clear without the need for words or wolf telepathy. In less than a minute, twenty-one people—twenty-one naked people—stand in front of me. I wait for them to grab clothes before I clear my throat and start.

"Okay, let's get this over with."

Esther steps forward. As a woman, she's intimating. Late thirties with jet black hair down to her waist and legs that go on forever, I think I can count the number of times I've seen her smile on one hand. She's powerful and forthright. Her beauty in human form is nothing compared to that as a wolf, when she's nothing short of mesmerising. The deep black of her fur is accentuated by a pure white streak that goes all the way down the ridge of her back. I knew she'd be the first to speak. She always is. Then it'll be one of the men and, after that, it'll descend into the usual chaos, and I can walk off and forget all this nonsense for another few weeks.

"This has gone on long enough," she says, in her broad Scottish accent. "This pack needs an alpha."

At least they're not pussyfooting around this time. Neither am I.

"I hate to state the obvious, but this is not a pack. It's only the left-over remnants on one—just twenty-four of us."

My words come out harsher than I'd planned, but we've had this conversation so many times, I'm tired of it.

"We *are* a pack," Esther continues.

"A pack is not defined by its size."

George starts talking now. He's always there, right by her side. At first, I thought they were an item, but I've discovered that's not the case, although I've not sifted through anyone's mind to find out exactly what their relationship is. I understand the need for privacy more than anyone.

"It's defined by the loyalty the members have to one another and to their alpha," he adds.

"Everyone here will follow you, Naz," Lou says with feeling. "You're a born leader. It's in your blood."

Tension ripples through the group. There's an unspoken rule among them that no-one brings up anything to do with my mother in front of me. I'm not sure why. Maybe they think it would be upsetting. Or perhaps it's because of the way I've lashed out at Calin for hiding her death from me, and they'd rather not risk being on the receiving end of that. But Lou doesn't follow the rules like the others do, where I'm concerned. And as she's the one who's going to have to deal with the fallout of this meeting going south again, I don't blame her for pulling out all the stops to try and make me change my mind.

She's not done yet.

"I know this is not what you planned, Naz. None of us did. And maybe you don't see yourself as Alpha, but no one is expecting you to get everything right straight away. Besides, that's not what being the Alpha is about. It's about having someone we can trust to guide our decisions, to bring the group's ideas together. This is what it comes down to. We trust you."

"I'm sorry," I say. "But the answer is still no, and it will always be no. I am not an alpha. And as for all that it-runs-in-my-veins nonsense, you're probably right. My mother was a great alpha. And look at what happened to her. If you really trust me the way you say you do, then perhaps you should when I say this is a terrible idea."

With my piece said, I consider the discussion over and turn to go back into the house before all the bickering begins when, out of the corner of my eye, I notice a flash of colour. The others spot it too. A blur of amber against the brown foliage. All attention now moves from me as we wait for her to reach us.

Chrissie. My mother's best friend and Beta of North Pack. This was before Juliette sided with the vampires, my mother was killed and most of her pack was forced into submission and taken down to South Pack. She'd reluctantly taken on the role of Alpha to those who'd escaped Juliette's clutches and led them, with Calin's help, to Lithuania, where they'd saved Oliver and me from Rey.

Since then, she's been trying to relieve herself of the responsibility. I can't say that I blame her.

As she reaches the garden, she turns back to human. The amber fur is gone, and in its place, grey hair flows down her back. Lou runs to meet her mother, embracing her briefly before Chrissie addresses everyone. Silence falls and we wait to hear what she has to tell us.

"I've heard from Adam," she says. "He's sent us the location of another nest."

4

In an instant, the mood goes from disappointment to excitement as energetic chatter ensues. Those who'd managed to find clothes are stripping off again, ready to change back to wolf, to run and deal with the latest vampire nest that's been discovered.

I've never met this Adam who is risking so much for us. He was one of my mother's pack. He decided not to resist Juliette but follow her, with the sole intention of feeding us intelligence whenever he could. Information such as the whereabouts of groups of rogue vampires, so that we could destroy them. I'd hoped that the nest we'd just eliminated in Klaipėda had been a random one-off, created by another crazed rogue, but that's evidently not the case. From what Adam has been able to find out, it seems very clear that one person is behind it all. Polidori.

"Where is it?" Esther asks, immediately making her way to Chrissie.

The noise subsides.

The older wolf grabs a long robe, handed to her by Lou, and slips it over her head. Esther doesn't give her time to dress properly before continuing to bombard her with questions.

"Did he say how big it is? How many days do you think it will take us to get there?"

"It's in Bratislava. A long trip. I don't know the exact numbers, but it's a large nest."

Excitement erupts again.

"We'll leave tonight."

"We need to eat first."

There's such a cacophony of voices, they can't possibly hear one another, and it's clear that no one has actually thought this through.

"Hold on!" I shout above the din. "No one is going anywhere!"

Silence falls again, as every pair of eyes turns to me.

"You don't want to be Alpha," Esther says. "You just said so. We can go wherever we want. Particularly if it means we get to kill some more vampire scum."

"No, you can't," I respond. "Not if you want to keep Adam safe."

A murmur rumbles through the group.

"We need to think about this logically," I continue. "We've attacked and destroyed nests at the last two locations he's learnt about. That was risky enough. If we're not careful, he may fall under suspicion. Juliette isn't stupid. She might already feel there's someone in her pack disclosing information. This could even be a test. We need to give this one a miss. Lie low for a couple of months."

"A couple of months!" someone calls out.

"He's telling us this so that we *can* do something about it. He knows the risks," adds another.

"He's passing us this intelligence so that we can *decide* whether to act, not leap blindly," I snap back. "And it's not just him who's at risk here. It's all of us. If Juliette suspects a leak, then any of the locations he sends us to could unknowingly be a trap. We need to take our time and think this over carefully."

The murmur has changed to what sounds like agreement. At least I hope it has. Some of these wolves are twice my age, yet at times it feels like I'm trying to manage a university dorm. Fight first. Think later. Not that I want to intervene the way an alpha would. I just want to stop them from getting themselves and the rest of us killed.

"What about that other place?" Esther speaks up. "The one I told you I smelt when I was on the run after Juliette's attack, before I met up with the rest of you. That was nearly six months ago now, and Adam hasn't ever mentioned it. If we target that, it could throw her off the scent. It would look like we're hitting places at random. Besides, it's only a couple of days run from here."

"We're not attacking any nests anywhere, no matter who's located them. No missions. Not now. We are lying low. Staying safe. That's the plan."

"It's sounds like the plan is to hide, if you ask me," someone pipes up.

A flicker of fear flashes across Lou's face, and the look in her eye is begging me not to erupt. But seriously, of all the stupid things to stay.

"Yes," I spit, marching through the crowd so I can look the person straight in the eye.

His name is Eric. He's a young wolf. He'd have to be to say something so witless.

"Yes, we *are* hiding. That's exactly what we're doing. We're hiding so that we can stay alive. We're hiding so that Juliette and the vampires don't kill us, or worse. We cannot win this right now. We don't even know exactly what we're fighting yet."

"This is not how wolves are supposed to act."

"You're joking, right? This is exactly how you were behaving when I met you, or have you forgotten already? Can you not remember what my mother gave her life for? Because I do. She was protecting you from an existence like they have in Juliette's pack, with the danger of death around every corner. And this is how you honour her memory. By trying to get yourself and others killed, just because you enjoy a fight. Really respectful. Well done."

Silence.

After a moment, Chrissie finally speaks.

"Narissa is right. We shouldn't risk this. It would be better to wait for Adam to pass us news on what their long-term plans are. For now, we stay here, where we're safe."

"Also, Régine's arranged pheasant for dinner. And roast potatoes," Lou pipes up in uber-cheerful mode, and even I can't help but smile.

She throws me a supportive glance. Sometimes I think I'd go mad if she wasn't here, although I'm probably already halfway there.

Slowly, chatter restarts and despite several glances in my

direction, no one addresses me again. Gradually, the crowd disperses, either as wolves into the forest or as humans into the house, until only Chrissie, Lou and I remain.

"Thank you," I say to them both.

"Don't be silly," Chrissie replies. You are right. But they feel useless, that's all. It was different back at the pack, before all this kicked off. They were happy then because they didn't think they had to do anything different. Now, they're frustrated at not being able to achieve something positive to change our situation."

"I get it," I say, and I do.

My own feelings of uselessness come from more than just the wolves' concerns. There's also Rey and the fact that I can't seem to do anything for her.

"How is Adam doing? Is he safe?" I ask.

"He thinks so. He says there are others on our side. Not just from our old pack but some of Juliette's, too."

I raise an eyebrow, expecting more.

"He doesn't want to share details, though. Doesn't want to put anyone else in danger. And it's difficult for him to be sure who is really for us, without risking outing himself, but he says there's a feeling of concern that the vampires have been allowed too much control over South Pack."

"But is anyone going to stand against her?"

She scrunches up her nose in a manner that says it all.

"They were all too scared to stand up to her before, and things have only got worse."

It's not the answer I wanted, but right now, I've got enough to deal with here without worrying about wolves I've never met.

"Okay. Well, for now, our priority has to be finding out what Polidori is up to. Keep me informed. I'm going for a run. Lou, you want to come?"

Her brow wrinkles apologetically, and I think she's about to tell me she can't for some reason.

"You might have to delay it a bit longer," she says, nodding to a figure walking towards us.

5

Half of me wants to turn into the wolf and go. I can't believe Oliver's got anything good to tell me. But he's standing there, patiently waiting to talk to me, and given what he's probably been going through with Rey, it only feels right that I speak to him.

"Do you have a minute?" he asks.

"I guess."

"Great, shall we go inside and talk?"

It's a rhetorical question, as he's already turning to walk back into the house. Lou offers me a sympathetic smile and I try to reciprocate, but I've not got enough energy left. Knowing I don't have much choice, I trudge after him, past the winding oak staircase, the dining room and kitchen, too. He's heading to the study, where we always go for private conversations.

For Régine's sake, we've tried to limit how much space we take up, but she doesn't seem to mind in the least. Her bedroom and bathroom are in the west wing of the chateau, and she's got her own snug there, too. We've agreed that her area is out of bounds, and so far, the arrangements seem to be working.

Apart from the huge house, she has a number of cottages on her land. We must have passed half a dozen on our runs, all in need of a lick of paint and a bit of TLC but in far better condition than some of the places Oliver and I stayed on our travels. When we first arrived, I suggested we make use of those, but Régine wasn't having any of that. She liked the company, she said. Maybe I should check in with her again. She might be having second thoughts after having all of us here for so long.

The study is around the same size as the living room in Oliver's London flat. An impressive mahogany writing desk sits in front of a tall bay window, and there are half-a-dozen chairs: a large high-backed one behind the desk, and two smaller ones in front of it, as if ready for a meeting. Then, along the book-lined walls are three tub chairs. The cream fabric is worn in places, the patterns faded or rubbed away from years of use, but all are comfy, and I've lost plenty of hours there, knees tucked under my chin, reading various volumes from Régine's vast collection. It reminds me of when I was at university, studying literature, which feels like a lifetime ago.

Apart from my little sanctuary upstairs and the bathroom with its view out over the lake, the study is my next-favourite place, but when Oliver pushes open the door and I see the figure sitting there, my stomach drops. An ambush.

"What's he doing here?" I demand.

Calin is in one of the chairs in front of the desk, one of the hard, uncomfortable ones. That's something, at least.

"We need to talk about Rey," Oliver replies. "This concerns him, too."

"I don't see why. He's nothing to do with her."

"Please, Naz. Just come in and listen."

There was a time when simply being in the same room on our own together would be enough to have Calin and me tearing the clothes off each other. I remember how it felt, wanting to run my fingers over every part of his body, draw in every scrap of his scent and taste. Does he still have that same desire now? I immediately shake away the thought. What does it matter how he feels about me? He lied. He hid a truth from me that was mine to know.

"So?" I say, in a tone that's clear how I'm feeling. I want to get this over and done with as soon as possible. "What is it? Did she tell you something? Did you get anywhere?"

Oliver shakes his head, and I feel a disappointment I wasn't expecting. We've had these conversations so many times, hoping that maybe soon we'd get lucky, that we'd find the key to whatever's keeping her the way she is. I'm not saying I thought nectarines would be the answer to our problem, but I guess I was hoping, like him, that they might trigger something. Anything.

"I don't think it's helping, keeping her confined," he says. "She can't do magic, but it's getting us nowhere."

"I just don't understand," I reply. "How did she change so much? It's like she's not even the same person."

"I suspect she is the same person," Calin speaks for the

first time since we entered the room. "But just all the bad bits."

His unblinking eyes linger on me for a moment before returning to Oliver. I feel their absence as much as I felt their presence.

"What do you mean?" he asks.

"This is only speculation," Calin replies, "but we can surmise that the vampires would have only given her access to the spells that they wanted her to perform for them. Ones that would benefit them."

"Like stopping wolves transforming so they could kill them," I say.

"Exactly or blocking the sun to give them free rein outside. Those are dark spells – black magic, in fact. While I'm not an expert, I believe to achieve it would require a witch to draw upon the darkest depths within herself and magnify what she finds there, if you will. The more Rey did this, the more it became part of her, until her true personality had been eclipsed."

It makes about as much sense as anything does in a world where I'm a werewolf, the person who was my best friend is a witch, and I have unresolved feelings for a one-hundred-and-twenty-year-old vampire.

"So, we need to access the white magic in her?" Oliver asks, looking to both of us for an answer.

When we can't give one, he carries on.

"Think about it. Witches were also known for the good they could do. So, although there are harmful spells and black magic, there must also be good spells and white magic. Plus, we know that, back in the day, they wanted to destroy the vampires, which means there must be a load of spells to that effect.

"So, what we need to do is find a good witch who could help us with all that, right?" My voice is laden with sarcasm. "You think that's going to be easy? Remember, before Rey was taken by the vampires, she was trying to do exactly that herself. She spent over a year searching for any hint that there was someone else like her out there, and she came back with nothing. Even if there are any, we have no idea how to go about tracking them down or how long it would take. I don't believe Rey has that kind of time left."

"No, you're right," Oliver says. "But I don't think we need a witch."

"What do you mean?"

"We just need the spells. We just need the grimoires. And we know there's more than one place we can get them."

6

What started out as a discussion has turned into a full-blown row, and I'm the one doing most of the shouting.

"You are both out of your minds. This is a no. A complete no."

"But it makes sense," Oliver argues. "The vampires aren't witches. They can't do magic. They would have had to give Rey the spells they wanted her to cast and made her repeat them. That's what Tamsin, that old witch she killed, was doing for her, when she was teaching Rey, right? We can do that. The grimoire Rey and I found way back when she first discovered her powers was written in Lithuanian. I speak Lithuanian. All I need to do is give Rey the right spells. This could work."

"And you can tell black magic from white magic spells, can you?"

"Well, I guess if it talks about making flowers appear, as

opposed to causing people to burst into flames, it should be fairly easy to distinguish."

I honestly can't believe he thinks this is a serious proposition. He's the more rational one of the two of us, although since he decided to try his hand at cage fighting, I'm starting to wonder. I get he's desperate, but he seems to have forgotten how dangerous this all is. We only escaped from whatever horrors Rey had planned for us because Calin and the wolves turned up and saved our skins. She's now a killer. We saw that for ourselves. Whatever we do, we can't risk making that side of her even more powerful. It seems as if Calin and Oliver are each too busy trying to prove they're in charge to think logically.

"Blackwatch made copies of all the grimoires they found, before handing them over to the vampires, and put them on their computer system," Oliver says. "If I could just gain access—"

"No. Blackwatch knows you're helping me," I say. "And in case you forgot, the Head of Blackwatch murdered my mother. It's too dangerous."

"Then I'll go," Calin says. "Not to Blackwatch. I'll go to the Council building. All the original grimoires are in the vaults there. They'd be better than copies, anyway. We don't want to miss anything."

"Again, no. You are not going anywhere near the Vampire Council. Did you not hear Rey? She knew about you and me, which means they must, too. Besides, you've been absent way too long. Polidori will know you don't agree with whatever it is he's got planned. The minute they sniff you out, it would be the end."

"Naz, please, you need to reconsider. Rey is in a bad way. I know you think she's dangerous—and she is—but that's only half of the picture. When she doesn't think we're watching her, and her guard is down … it's almost like she's fading away. There's no light in her eyes. No life …"

He stops talking and shudders.

"I don't know how much longer she can keep going like this."

Clutching my head in my hands, I dig my nails into my scalp with frustration. Is this what life is now: playing Russian roulette with my friends' lives? Right now, they're all here and they're all alive. If one of them goes after those grimoires and I lose him, as well as Rey, well, it's just not worth the gamble.

"No," I say again, lifting my head to look at them both. "We're not risking it. Not 'til we know what Polidori is up to. Rey is safe, for the moment, and that's what matters."

I speak like the debate is over, but before I can leave, Calin is on his feet and appears in front of me with that annoying super-speed vampire move he does.

"Please, Narissa, think about it seriously. I can do this for her."

My eyes lock on his, something I've avoided doing for months now, for fear of the feelings that it might stir up. I see it all there in his expression, his hurt, his pain and his guilt. I see other things, too. Ones that make me want to push everything aside and pull him straight into my arms and then upstairs into my bed. Why? When I trusted him so completely, why would he hide my mother's death from me? Even if I wanted to forgive him, I don't think I ever could.

"You've done enough already," I say.

His eyes remain on mine a moment longer, then he nods and disappears out of the room.

I stand there in his wake, until Oliver's voice reminds me I'm not on my own.

"You should ease up on him, you know."

"Sorry?"

I turn to see his face etched with concern.

"I think it's been long enough now. The guy's suffering. I'm not saying you should go back to … you know … but you could at least be civil to him."

"He lied to me, Oliver. He knew my mother was dead, and he let me go on for months without knowing."

"He lied to protect you, that's all, because he didn't want you to do anything rash. He wanted to keep you safe."

"Wow," I say, flopping down into one of the armchairs. "This is a turnaround. I thought you hated the guy."

"This is not about my opinion of him," he replies. "It's just that I get where he was coming from, and so should you."

"What's that supposed to mean?"

His eyebrows arch with a mixture of disbelief and confusion.

"You're joking. You're the queen of keeping secrets to protect people."

"I *was*. And that was only once, when I stole from you."

"How about the time you pretended to be a blood

donor and let a vampire feed from you? Or when you were on the run from Joe, after you'd stolen money from him? And let's not forget when you and Rey didn't tell me about your plans to go to the Blood Bank—"

"All right, I get it. I'm a terrible person." I lift my hands in surrender.

"That's not what I meant," he says, lowering his volume as he sits down next to me. "What I'm saying is that you should understand how people can make the wrong decision when it comes to protecting others they care about. You of all people should be able to empathise with that."

I can feel my teeth grinding. I'm exasperated beyond measure but, deep down, I know he's right. That's the thing about Oliver. He's too damned good to be true. Even though I know exactly how he feels about my past relationship with Calin, he still manages to do the right thing. I guess that's why he's probably the best person I know.

"You'd never do something like that to me, though. You'd never lie to me."

"I would do anything, if it meant keeping you safe," he says.

There's a change in atmosphere between us, to something I've managed to avoid since we've been here at the house. Before we attacked the rogues and Rey reappeared, Oliver and I shared a drunken kiss. Our first kiss, drunken or otherwise. And it was good. Magical. No, maybe that's the wrong word. Tingly. I've found myself thinking back to it, repeatedly. But what with a best friend locked up and a pack of wolves to keep in line, there hasn't been that much time to ponder on my love life. And that's before I even touch on the subject of the vampire who sleeps across the hall from me.

"We'll talk about us," I say, taking his hand to ease the tension a little, "just as soon as we get things sorted with Rey. We'll find time."

"There's no rush," he says, with a smile that makes my heart flutter. "I'm not going anywhere."

He stands and kisses me on the top of my head.

"Well, I'd better go and clean up. You know how upset Régine gets if we don't dress properly for dinner," he says, and the moment is gone.

7

It could be the dining room from a Jane-Austen period drama. The table is so long, it's big enough to take all of us wolves, plus Calin, Oliver and Régine and still have room to spare. I've no idea where you'd buy one like this these days, but I'm pretty sure you wouldn't get one delivered by Amazon. Above us are two large chandeliers. The candles have been swapped for electric bulbs, probably years ago, but the beautiful cut-glass prisms disperse the light and make it flicker as if there are actual flames up there.

The first time we sat down like this, Régine was so appalled at our attire that she insisted we all head upstairs to her vast wardrobes and change before she'd allow us to eat. She could have easily had a riot on her hands, but we were all so exhausted, and the food smelt so good, none of us had the energy to protest. I thought it was a ridiculous idea, until I saw the clothes.

I still don't know how she spent her time during her

early years, but from what was in front of us that evening, I would say clothes shopping featured heavily. With walk-in wardrobes and dressing rooms the size of the average lounge, she had more than enough to kit us all out in formal dinner wear, including dozens of men's tuxedos and dinner jackets. On that first night, despite everything we'd been through, we girls found ourselves laughing as we tried on silk dresses with trains and feathers boas, tiptoeing around in high heels and helping each other pull up the zippers on items that hadn't seen the light of day in decades. The next day, she insisted that Henri go to the nearest town and purchase a more suitable selection for us all. Occasionally though, we still play at dressing up for dinner. It seems to lift everyone's spirits and is definitely appropriate when Henri has cooked up a special feast. It gives us the chance to switch off for a little while.

Tonight, I've chosen a black-and-silver flapper dress with a fringed hem and crystal beadwork. It's one I liked the look of when I saw Lou wearing it a few weeks ago but had forgotten about until I headed upstairs this afternoon.

As always, there's more than enough food. Platters of meat—including half-a-dozen pheasants—vegetables and roast potatoes have been laid out for us, although my eyes fall first on the small glass of red liquid in front of Calin.

I haven't asked where he's been getting blood from since we came here, and he's barely left the house. In London, it had been provided by Blackwatch. Later … well, that was how we met, after all: me offering him mine. I know he wouldn't ask any of the wolves for a donation, which means either Régine or her butler, Henri, are the donors and I'm not sure how I feel about that. Either way, his attention is solely on her at dinner, and it reminds me of the story she likes to tell about how they first met. It must feel special for her, having someone pay so much attention to you, as if you're their entire world. I should know.

"Now, that looks tasty," Esther says, pulling out a chair and sitting down next to me. "Absolutely delicious, in fact."

"Well, dig in," I say. "There's plenty here."

"Oh, I wasn't talking about the food."

Her eyes flicker across to where Oliver is sitting, next to Chrissie and George. He's dressed in a simple tuxedo, though without a bow tie, which seems to be his preferred style. His top button is undone, and there's a shadow of stubble on his face.

"That's what's whetting my appetite," she says.

My hand grips my fork tighter, and I impale a parsnip with more force than I'd intended. I don't know if she's trying to get a rise out of me or not, but either way, I decide not to pass comment.

"So, tell me, what's the deal with you two. I mean, I've hung back, but I'm getting thirsty. And it doesn't help when he gets all dressed up like that."

"Oliver is off limits," I say firmly, through gritted teeth.

"Off limits, as in you don't want to share but actually he is fair game, or off limits as in you're telling me, as Alpha, to stay away from him?"

Damn her. I should have known there'd be an ulterior motive for this banter. She's never shown the slightest interest whatsoever in him before, and I'd bet my dinner she's not bothered now, either. It's just another attempt to get me to commit to a role I don't want and shouldn't be trusted with anyway. I'm holding my cutlery so firmly, my knuckles have turned white. The merry chatter around us contrasts markedly with the animosity I'm feeling towards her.

"Oliver has a lot on his plate at the minute. He's trying to get Rey sorted out and doesn't need any distractions. But then again, I guess it's up to him how he spends his spare time."

"So, you wouldn't mind if I take him for the occasional ride? Provided he isn't distracted from his work, that is."

The wolf in my head growls, desperate for me to put her in her place. But what place is that? We're both just wolves. I have no authority over her, unless I decide to take it, permanently.

"You do whatever you want," I say, staring at my plate as I stab again, this time missing a roast potato, hitting the porcelain and producing an unpleasant scraping noise.

"Fantastic," she says and stands up.

Taking her plate with her, she moves around the table and whispers something in George's ear, at which point he gets up, brings his plate over and sits down next to me. Brilliant Naz. Bloody brilliant.

The rest of dinner is uneventful. Occasionally, Régine's attention turns to one of us and she asks if we're enjoying our stay and if we've visited a certain place in the grounds, such as the grotto or the amphitheatre.

"It's a full moon tonight," Lou announces. "After dinner, I'm going for a run to the river—maybe offer a prayer to Eve, for old time's sake—if anyone fancies it?"

This is met with murmurs of agreement.

"What about you, Naz? Do you want to come too?"

"Maybe. I'll think about it."

Her eyes flicker with a hint of sadness, but her lips smile in a way that tells me she understands. I've been running with the pack plenty since we came here, particularly on the missions to destroy the two vampire nests Adam told us about. I enjoyed the sense of purpose, with something to focus on. For a while, I was able to forget all the things that are wrong in my life. But runs like Lou's suggesting now, where we simply kick back, let loose and flow with the earth, those I haven't managed. I didn't do that when I was with them in Scotland, either. There wasn't enough time. One of the few occasions I ran at all there was with Freya, my mother. It's what remains of her pack that I'm with right now. Her family, not mine. The idea of joining them tonight just serves to remind me.

After the main course, comes a bread pudding that is so rich and creamy, I can only manage half a bowlful, although this is more than our hostess who just sips at a glass of brandy. As we are finishing, still busy talking, she gets up from her seat.

"I think I would quite like to see this full moon myself," she says. "Calin, would you care to accompany me on a promenade?"

"It would be my pleasure," he says, standing and taking her hand.

"Then I will bid you all a goodnight. And, although it pains me to ask this, if you could take your dishes through to the kitchen yourselves, it would be a great help to Henri.

He, like some of us others here, is not as young as he used to be."

We thank her and bid her a goodnight in return, and shortly, the wolves start to leave, too. Across the table, Lou and Chrissie are in a heated conversation. If I had to guess, I'd say it was about their missing family member, Art. Mother and daughter are so similar and rarely fight, but given the pain he has caused them, it's unsurprising. I sometimes find myself thinking about him. He went willingly to Juliette's pack. I know that much. He's probably trying to work his way up the ranks there, despite the punishment injury inflicted on him by Chrissie.

Next to them, Esther has an arm draped around Oliver. I watch them for a while. It actually makes me smile. Poor old Oliver. He's so clueless. Not as to what she's after—anyone could tell that from a mile off—but how to react. His body is rigid, his face strained in a forced smile. It could be amusing to watch this go on a little longer. Then again, he might eventually decide he likes the attention.

"Oliver, why don't you help me carry some of these dishes through to the kitchen?" I say. "Help Henri a bit."

I fix my gaze on Esther, who smirks at me like I've finally risen to the bait she's put out. There again, maybe I have.

"I need to pop upstairs before we leave," Lou says, getting to her feet. "I hate changing when I've got makeup on. It mats my fur and is a complete mess when I turn back again. See you all out there in twenty?" she asks, not really expecting anyone to answer, as they all mill around.

"Don't worry about that," Oliver says as people go to

tidy away their plates. "Naz and I have got this, haven't we?"

"Sure."

Before she leaves, Chrissie comes over and places a gentle kiss on my cheek.

"You know, you're always welcome to join us, but there's no rush. Your mother would be very proud of what you're doing. Of everything you've done."

"I hope so," I reply.

"I know it."

The last wolf to leave is Esther.

"I'll be back about two," she says to Oliver, as if I'm not even there. "If you fancy, I could always come up and warm your bed."

I watch as a thousand shades of crimson appear on his cheeks.

"Uhm, well … that's very nice of you … but maybe another night?"

"I'll hold you to that," she says, before disappearing with a sashay that makes his eyes bug.

"Wow," he says after she's gone. "These wolf women don't go for subtle, do they?"

"Some of us do," I reply. "Esther, on the other hand, is very single minded. Tends to set her sights on something and doesn't give up until she gets it."

"By *something*, you mean me?"

I laugh at his discomfort. I had actually been thinking of the way she's been badgering me to take on the role of Alpha. Given that she's not shown any interest in Oliver before tonight, I'm not sure which of us her behaviour has been aimed at.

"Don't worry," I say with a smirk. "I'll protect you."

Together, we ferry the serving dishes, plates, cutlery and glasses into the kitchen, where Henri loads the massive dishwasher. I wonder what he thinks about all this. He must know a good deal. Régine trusts him implicitly and so does Calin, so that's good enough for us. I also doubt if an elderly man would have any intention of getting on the wrong side of a bunch of werewolves who keep company with a vampire and a psychotic witch, even if the latter is safely locked away.

"I think we have the house to ourselves tonight," Oliver says when the job's finally done. "The wolves are out running; Calin is out with Régine; and Henri looks like he'll be dead to the world as soon as his head hits the pillow."

"I think you're right," I respond.

He looks at me and smiles, and a swarm of butterflies takes flight in my stomach.

8

I don't know why I suddenly feel this way. One minute we were standing there quite normally, stacking up dirty plates for the next run of the dishwasher in the morning, and then everything changed.

"Naz …"

"Don't …" I say, the butterflies moving faster.

"Naz, there's something I need you to know."

"I do already. I heard you before we were rescued, remember? But I realised before that. You must have known I did."

He frowns momentarily, but I guess there's nothing more that needs to be said. I know he loves me—the good bits and the bad. He always did but never said the words out loud until he thought it was the end. He called out for me then, just as I had thought of him, in Scotland, when I believed my time was up. He looks uncomfortable and shuffles his feet.

"We should talk about what we do now," he says.

CHAPTER 8

Talking. That's all we seem to do. Talk with the wolves. Talk about Rey. Talk about what happens next.

"How about we don't," I suggest.

"No?" He looks confused.

"No. How about we have that sober kiss you promised me, instead?"

For months, I've wondered if the intensity of that first kiss was simply a hyped-up memory caused by too much alcohol and not enough sleep. But the moment I move towards him, I know it's not true. A tingling is spreading through me, and my breathing is growing shallower and faster by the second. Thoughts of Calin flicker in the back of my mind, but I immediately push them away.

"I don't want you to do anything you'll regret," he says, now only a whisper away.

"I don't think I'm going to regret this at all," I respond.

Our lips meet, and it's like a pressure valve releasing in my chest. I want more; I need more, but he pulls away and brushes my hair behind my ears.

"Naz, I'm so sorry. I just wanted to protect you."

"I don't need protecting."

My hands are fiddling with his belt buckle. It loosens, and my fingers reach for the top of his trousers.

"Not here. Upstairs. We do this properly."

I don't even know what that means, but right now, I don't care. He takes my hand and leads me out of the kitchen.

"Are you sure?" he asks again when we reach my door.

"You know, I'm starting to think you don't want to do this," I say with a smile.

"Well, I should probably reassure you about that then, shouldn't I?" he replies with a grin.

He pushes me into the bedroom and closes the door.

The light is off, but the full moon shines through the window, casting everything in a watery glow. Like everything else here, the room is extravagant, with a large ornate mirror and a fresco of cherubs playing amongst clouds, on the ceiling. But the bed is simply a wooden frame with a soft mattress. As I fiddle with the zip of my dress, Oliver turns me around, then moves my hair to the side and kisses the base of my neck once and then again.

The last person I did this with was Calin, in the wooden shack at North Pack. We went from kissing to ripping each other's clothes off in a matter of seconds, and I can't help but make comparisons. The situations couldn't be more different, and yet I'm just as breathless, just as hot, just as desperate for him to lay me down on the bed and take me. But I know I'm going to have to be patient.

"Tell me," he says, slowly drawing my zip down. My dress slips from my shoulders and falls to the floor.

"Tell you what?" I whisper.

"Tell me what you want, what you need."

"Just to forget everything else for a while."

I DON'T KNOW HOW LONG IT LASTED. ALL I DO KNOW IS, once it was over, I realised I'd never experienced anything like it before. The tenderness. The consideration. The way his eyes stayed locked on me the whole time, as he matched his rhythm to mine, as I gripped the mattress, trying desperately to stifle the screams that threatened to explode from me and my muscles spasmed.

"Whatever you need," Oliver whispered to me "I'll do it. Whatever you need."

"Just don't let go of me," I replied, almost choking on tears I had no explanation for. And he didn't. As we fell asleep, he kept his arms wrapped tightly around me. Cocooning me from the world outside.

The moon is fading, and the night is disappearing with the first rays of sun, as I roll out from under him. My body is sticky with the sweat of our exertions. In truth, I would have stayed there a lot longer, if it were not for an overwhelming thirst. As good as Henri's food is, the richness always leaves me needing a drink in the night.

"Hey," he says, his hand reaching out and grabbing me. "Where are you going? You're not running off and leaving me already, are you?"

He looks even cuter than ever, with his face squashed up against his pillow and his hair crumpled at funny angles.

"You're in my bed, so I would have to kick you out if I wanted rid of you."

"And do you?" he asks, propping himself up on an elbow. "Want to kick me out?"

"I haven't made up my mind yet," I joke but see a hint of worry appear on his face.

"You know I only want to keep you safe, don't you?" he says. "I just want you to be happy."

"I know."

"And that I'd never hurt you. Not deliberately."

I tilt my head, trying to read him.

"I thought you'd worry about me breaking your heart."

"After a performance like that," he smiles, "I'd say you must be smitten. Admit it."

Leaning in, I place a kiss on his lips. It feels such a natural thing to do. Like this is how it's always been.

"I'll need to take you for another test run, just to be sure."

His grin stretches. "I'm sure that can be arranged."

He goes to pull me back onto the bed, but I slip from his grasp. I grab my dressing gown from the back of the door.

"I must get some water."

9

With so many of us here, the house is rarely silent, yet as I come down to the kitchen, the stairs creak noisily beneath my feet in the stillness. Plates are stacked as they were when Oliver and I went up, and the fridge is still full when I check it. The wolves must still be out, I decide, or it would have been ransacked by now. After long runs, they do a pretty good job of polishing off whatever food is handy. If Régine ever decides to bill us for everything we've eaten since moving in here, we would be screwed, to say the least.

I find a clean glass, fill it with water from the tap and down half of it in one go.

I had sex with Oliver. I say to myself and can't help smiling.

I had sex with Oliver. I think again. *And it was good. So good.*

Alone here in the darkness, I feel myself blushing, which is absurd. It's crazy that we put off something that was so inevitable for so many years. Each of us worrying that it would change things between us. But why on earth? If this version of us doesn't work out, we can go back to the way we were. I don't see how that would be a problem. After all, he and Rey had a friends-with-benefits relationship for a long time. Why couldn't we do the same?

Thinking of Rey takes my mind to places I hadn't expected it to go. Her and Oliver for a start. I know that they messed around for years, but I'd never thought that deeply about it or wondered how he felt about it. I know her side of things. Right from the off, she insisted they weren't a couple and neither of them had any desire to be one. They were just two friends who lived mad lives and occasionally found release in one another's beds. And from the way they interacted, that seemed to be the case.

So, what does that make me and Oliver? Distraction from these crazy times is definitely something I've needed, but it seems that he's always wanted much more. What if I'm not able to give him that? What if, for me, it's just good sex and nothing else? One minute I'm feeling on top of the world and the next I'm doubting myself again. Am I ready for more commitment? I'm not, am I? No, of course it can't work.

Shit.

I pace up and down with the now empty glass in my hand. What I need is someone to talk to, but who? Lou's been trying to get me to make up with Calin since we first got here. The irony hadn't escaped my notice considering how terrified she was of him at first. I guess arranging a private jet for our escape helped her see him in a different light. But she doesn't seem to understand that no matter

CHAPTER 9

what I may have felt for him before, I can't even look at him without feeling betrayed now. They say there's a fine line between love and hate and I know for certain I hate Calin for what he did and I'm not about to risk getting myself in a position where it might slip the other way, if it ever could.

It's what's going on with Oliver I need help with. Chrissie would be a good person to talk to, although she'd probably tell me to follow my heart, like my mother did once. But where is my heart leading me? I have no idea.

I need to speak to someone who really knows me. And not just me but Oliver, too.

I need to talk to Rey.

10

Part of me thinks this is a bad idea. Probably quite a large part. But then there's a flicker of hope in there, too. From what Oliver has said, the whole problem is getting through to her humanity. That's what the dark magic she's been doing has blocked, and that's what we need to find a way to release. Well, what's more human than talking about boyfriend problems? If anything is going to jerk her back into remembering life as it was before, surely it's got to be that.

I make my way out of the house via the back door and head around to the small brick lean-to. In my hand, I've got a plastic bowl containing left-over bread pudding from earlier. We've discovered she can't do anything much with plastic, but I don't risk cutlery. I'm optimistic, not stupid.

As I place my hand on the heavy bolt, my heart is thumping. I should turn around now. I should go back to my room with that glass of water I promised Oliver. We could pick up where we left off and I'll wait until a more sensible hour to talk to Rey, or come to my senses and stay out of her way altogether. But I want to try this. I'm sure it could be a way in.

"Are you planning on standing there all night, Narissa, or are you coming in to say hello?"

Her voice makes me jump so much, I nearly drop the bowl. She can sense I'm out here! I gulp. There's no point delaying this any longer. So, without allowing for any more time to second guess myself, I unbolt the door and step inside.

"Narissa, what a pleasant surprise."

There's something about the way she says my name. It's a bit like a cartoon snake might pronounce it, with too much emphasis on the S's. And Rey never called me Narissa before, only ever Naz. But this isn't the old Rey I'm talking to. I need to keep reminding myself of that.

She's slumped forward with her feet hanging off the edge of the bed. The bed that she sleeps and eats and even pisses on if there's no one here at the appropriate moment. Her shackles are long enough to give her a bit of movement but not a lot. I don't think I could have ever imagined keeping my worst enemy locked away like this, let alone my best friend. Yet here she is. With her head still down, she's observing me from beneath her fringe.

"I brought you some food," I say.

"A little late for room service, isn't it?"

"I was up."

"So I see. You've been avoiding me."

"That's because you've been trying to kill me."

She blinks and nods, and for an instant, I swear I can

see a sheen of tears across her eyes. Then it's gone, if it was ever there. She reaches out a hand for the bowl, stretching as far as the chains will allow, then holds it up to her nose and takes a deep sniff.

"Dessert. It's been a long time since I've had anything like this. I guess a spoon is out of the question."

"I didn't want to take any risks."

"Understandable."

Using a finger and thumb, she pinches off a corner of one of the firmer pieces and brings it to her lips. The next time, she breaks off a bigger bit, then a third and a fourth. She stops shovelling the pudding into her mouth for a moment and looks up, her eyes glimmering.

"This is really good," she says. "Thank you."

These few sentences represent the most civil conversation we've had in three months and it's certainly the longest she's gone without trying to hurt me. There's something different about her, too. A bit of colour in her cheeks, perhaps.

When she's finished eating all she can with her fingers, she lifts the bowl and lets the rest of it run into her mouth. It's not elegant and bits dribble down her chin and land on her top. I instinctively move to wipe them away, only to stop myself at the last moment and step back again. Bad things tend to happen when I get too close to Rey.

"It's okay," she says, as if reading my mind, then stretches out her hand with the empty bowl.

I remain where I am for a moment, then lean forward and take it.

"I'm assuming you didn't come here just to bring me a

midnight snack," she says. "I must admit, I'm a bit surprised. I've noticed you've pretty much given up on visiting me, but I guess abandoning me is your default position."

"I'm sorry; you're right. I don't come here much. We thought it was best for you if I stayed away."

"So why tonight?"

"I don't know," I say, but she sees right through me.

"Don't do that. Don't lie to me. You came to tell me something. I know that look, and I know you, Naz, remember."

Naz. A flicker of hope springs up, but I squash it down quickly. This could be nothing more than a trap, a trick to put me off my guard.

"I should go."

"Please, Naz. Stay. I want to hear about you. I miss you."

There it is again, but I can't let myself believe she's suddenly changed. I go to leave, but glancing back at her, I see it's more than just a sheen in her eyes. Tears have begun to escape and are trickling down her cheeks. What was it Oliver said about her fading? I can see it myself now.

"I ... I'm s-sorry," she says, her words coming in stuttering half breaths. "I want to control it. I do. But every time I think I've blocked it, it finds a way back in. I just want to feel normal again. I want things to go back to the way they were. I want us to be able to talk like we used to."

The pain in my chest is visceral. It feels like my heart is genuinely breaking. How did she end up like this? Of all the unfair things in the universe.

My back against the wall, I slide down to the floor, sitting on my hands to combat the urge to go and hug her. I can stay with her a little longer. I should stay while she's like this.

After a few moments, her tears subside. When she looks at me, there's the hint of a smile on her lips.

"So, are you going to tell me the real reason for this late-night visit or not?" she asks.

I hesitate, but this is why I came here in the first place.

"Oliver and I, we, well …"

I don't need to finish the sentence. Her eyes widen and her face breaks into a full smile, something not seen since we came here.

"Wow, so are congratulations in order?"

"It's all very new. Very, very new."

"Well, you know he's been in love with you since forever. I was starting to give up hope you'd ever get it together."

"I'm not sure you can actually call us *together*."

"Of course, you can. Wow," she says again, and even in this dim light, I can see the bleakness in her eyes has lifted a little. Not quite old Rey yet, but the glimmer of a hope. "I'll be honest, I didn't see that coming. After the last few months, I figured you'd end up with the vampire."

I'm thrown off guard for a second. Why would she say that? But then I remember, when she confronted us in Lithuania, she already knew about me and Calin. There seems no point in keeping any of the details from her.

"Well, the vampire has a nasty habit of lying to me."

"You mean about your mother being dead?"

The words come out so matter-of-factly, it's like a slap in the face.

"I didn't mention my mother to you," I say.

A small frown appears between her eyebrows.

"Not much to do these days but listen. Your little pups like to gossip. I think they forget I'm in here. Plus, Tamsin shared most of her visions with me. I wonder if I wasn't a bit hasty there, getting rid of her."

I feel a sudden chill.

"I should go," I say, standing up and reaching for the door handle. I don't know why, but my pulse has kicked up a notch.

"Of course, you should. Thank you again for the pudding."

I open the door, but as I'm about to step outside, she speaks again.

"Just one last thing before you go."

My heart is racing. Why am I suddenly so fearful? She's been completely civil to me and there's nothing she can use as a weapon. Yet I'm dreading what might come next.

"Sure," I say, trying to sound calm, despite my pulse hammering in my ears. "What is it?"

Her smile broadens as she looks at me with her big brown eyes.

"I just wonder why you won't forgive the vampire for lying to you about your mother's death, but Oliver gets a free pass for doing the exact same thing?"

"What?" My breath catches. "He didn't know Freya was dead."

"Did he not? Are you sure?"

My insides are churning. I turn away. I want to race back into the house and forget these last few minutes ever happened. But my eyes are drawn back to her. She's no longer slouching. She's sitting bolt upright, her arms wrapped around her knees. Her smile has morphed into that familiar dark sneer. She lifts a hand and gives a small wave.

"Bye, Narissa. It's been lovely talking with you."

11

As I bolt the door, I can't stop trembling. My legs have turned to water, and I have to rest my hands on the cold brick wall to stop myself from collapsing. Oliver knew my mother was dead. It can't be true. He couldn't have known and not told me. He couldn't have spent all that time promising me everything would be fine. She must be lying. That's what this Rey does. She twists things.

Still holding myself steady, I think of the glee in her eyes as she watched her words sink in. The look of triumph as she saw the damage they'd done. That was it all along. That nonsense, calling me *Naz,* like she used to, wasn't because she's getting better. It's because she wanted to inflict as much pain as possible. That's not Rey in there. It's some foul impostor who's determined to torment me. This thought brings me a modicum of comfort. Of course she'd lie, try to stir up trouble. It probably angered her to see me looking happy.

But if that's the case, if she is lying, why do I feel sick to my stomach? Is it possible she's the only one in this whole damned mess who's telling me the truth?

I make my way back through the kitchen. I grip the banister as I climb the stairs, my knuckles white and my palms growing slick with sweat. He'll be there, waiting for my return. I don't know which was the more stupid: giving in to whatever this is between us; or going to see Rey.

I reach my room, push the door open and step inside.

"What took you so long? I was about to come looking for you," he says, his sleepy eyes smiling at me. He bites his bottom lip and pulls the bedsheet aside. "It's hours until we need to get up. Come back to bed."

I stay where I am, my throat tight and my chest pounding. His smile starts to fade. His eyes go to my hands which are clutched at my sides.

"Naz, are you okay? What happened to the water? I thought you went to fetch us a drink?"

I shake my head, almost lost for words.

"Did you know? Did you know Freya was dead, all along?"

He sits up, pulling the sheet back over himself as the colour dissolves from his cheeks.

"You've been talking to Calin, haven't you? What did he say?"

Of all the answers he could have given, I wasn't expecting that one. He didn't even try to hide his lies. Tears build in my eyes as I feel my heart breaking. I'd been holding out the hope that Rey was lying, but even if he hadn't spoken a word, the truth is there in his face, as clear as day.

CHAPTER 11

"You knew. You knew, and you didn't tell me."

He leaps out of bed, grabbing the sheet around his waist, but when he reaches me, I push him away.

"Naz, it's not that simple."

"You let me believe she was still alive. You listened to me talking about her. And you knew. You knew all along."

He looks distraught, but I don't care. I couldn't give a shit if he's hurting right now. He tries to approach me again, and I bat him away once more.

"I wanted to tell you, but he made me promise not to."

"Promise?"

"I gave him my word."

I shake my head, unable to believe what I'm hearing.

"This isn't like keeping a promise in the playground, Oliver. This is my life."

"I understand. But Calin—"

"I'm talking about you! You, Oliver! This has nothing to do with him. You kept it from me. You lied to me day in and day out. You're supposed to be my friend."

My words cut through us both, but they're the truth.

"I am, Naz. You know I'd never do anything to hurt you."

He reaches out for my hand, but I snatch it away from him. Just the thought of his skin on mine makes me recoil.

"Please, Naz. Come back to bed and we'll talk. I'll explain everything. I swear I didn't want to lie to you. It tore me up inside. How do I make this better? Tell me what I should do. How to make it right."

"You can't."

Blinking away tears, I race out of the bedroom and

onto the landing. He calls after me as he stumbles around, probably trying to get some clothes on. But I'm not in the mood for listening. All I care about is getting away.

Picking up the pace, I start down the stairs, just as the front door sweeps open and several people walk in, chattering to one another. The wolves are just returning. The sun has started to rise. It must have been a good run if they've stayed out this long. I should have gone with them. I should have stayed away from Oliver and Rey and this whole damned mess. I sense a growl of agreement from the wolf in the back of my head. But even a run wouldn't free me from this anger. I'm furious at both of them, Calin and Oliver. And Rey, too. No, none of this is on her. But those two … they're no better than each other. No wonder Oliver was telling me to forgive Calin this morning. All that bullshit about him just trying to protect me and only doing what he thought was right at the time. He wasn't talking about Calin; he was talking about himself.

"Naz, are you okay?" Lou asks.

I hadn't noticed she was one of the group, which is now blocking the stairs and my route away from Oliver and his lies.

"You don't look right."

"I need to go for a run," is all I can manage.

"Well, we can come with you, if you like?"

There's worry etched on her face. She looks to the others for confirmation. They nod immediately, and I realise Esther is there too. Esther. It seems almost fated.

"Esther," I say, suddenly more focused than I've been in

a long time, "that vampire, the one you're convinced Juliette's pack doesn't know about. Where did you say it was?"

"Just across the border into Italy, near Turin."

"And you could get us there?"

A smile creeps across her face.

"Of course I could."

"Great," I say, whipping off my T-shirt and draping it around the newel post.

"We're leaving now."

12

Oliver

Shit. Shit, shit, shit. I knew. I knew, without a shadow of a doubt, that this was going to come back and bite me. I knew from the first time he told me to lie to her it was a stupid idea, but I went along with it like a bloody idiot. And here I am, on my own again, only hours after finally holding in my arms the one girl I could actually see a future with. How the hell did it go like this? How did I mess this up so royally?

"Fuck!" I pick up a pillow and hurl it across the bedroom. "You're a fucking fool. Why didn't you tell her before?"

Talking to myself doesn't help, but I don't know what else to do. What really pisses me off is that I genuinely wanted to tell her. Every day, the moment I wake up, it's the first thought it my head. Yesterday evening, I so nearly did. When the wolves left for their run, Calin went off with Régine, and it was just me and her in the kitchen, I really thought I'd manage to get the truth out. But then I bottled it again.

By the time I'd grabbed my shorts and got to the top of the stairs, I could hear voices below. Lou and Esther. The wolves would have torn me apart if they'd found out how I'd hurt her. Not that I don't deserve it. But I'd at least like the chance to explain myself, first. So, I hung back and waited for them to move on, so I could get her on her own again, but then they left, with Naz in the lead. And now I'm feeling like the piece of shit I am.

For a while, I just sit in my room, staring out the window as the sun appears over the horizon. Wolves are milling around in the garden, but she's not one of them. Even from this distance, I'd recognise her out of all the others. She's like a beacon to me. Wolf or human, nothing else shines quite like her. Wherever she's gone, I guess she's not planning on returning anytime soon.

Tiredness is not something that affects me the way it does most people. It's down to the Blackwatch training. But that doesn't mean I don't feel heavy. Drained.

I realise that I never got that glass of water. My throat is parched and scratchy, half from the saltiness of last night's food but also from the tears I've shed because of my own stupidity. Pulling on a T-shirt, I head down to the kitchen. Having quenched my thirst, I prepare breakfast for Rey.

No one is allowed to see Rey without my approval. I'm the one who delivers her food and empties her slop bucket.

I'm the one who reads to her or brings her books in the hope she'll read them herself. It's not hard to maintain this discipline. Since their encounter with her at the abandoned house, the wolves have little desire to be anywhere near her.

I unbolt the door and step inside. It might be early, but Rey is already sitting in her chair. She's smiling and her eyes are gleaming. Odd.

"Oliver, good morning. Did you have a nice night?"

It all starts to fall into place.

"What have you done?"

I have no time for playing her games, and the way she's smirking now, tells me everything I need to know.

"Is everything okay?" she asks. "I thought I heard a little shouting a while back. It sounded like Narissa. I hope she's all right. She sounded a little upset."

"What did you tell her?"

I enunciate each word with such force I'm practically spitting. She feigns innocence for a moment longer, then drops her jaw in mock surprise.

"Oh, you mean about you knowing that her mother was dead all along. It was actually quite a sweet conversation, you know. I think she's finally got a bit of a thing for you. Or at least, she did have. That might have changed now she knows you were lying to her."

She's so calm, so at ease with the torment she's inflicting. How is it possible that someone can change completely in such a short space of time? It's as if her very soul has been reprogrammed.

"Why did you do this to us?"

"Oh, Olly, don't take things so personally. There are

plenty more fish in the sea. Or bitches in the pack if you prefer that metaphor."

For the first time since we brought her here, I want to wring her neck. I've been blaming myself for what happened in the forest, when she let the vampires nearly kill us. And I blamed myself and Naz for not looking for her after the events at the Blood Bank. But this. This is all on her.

"I thought you didn't care about what happened to us. For someone who's abandoned everything connected to her old life, you seem to be doing a great job meddling in it."

"Just because I have no desire to fall back into your mundane existence doesn't mean I don't want to have fun. And what can I say? My options for entertainment here are limited. But I do hope Naz is all right. Give her my regards when you see her again, won't you?"

It's as much as I can take. I toss her tray on the floor and leave. Her cackling reverberates around the walls as I slam the door closed and bolt it.

I think my morning can't get any worse, until I return to the kitchen and see who's standing there. Even in the dim light, with the curtains still drawn, he cuts an impressive figure.

"How are you feeling?"

He sounds genuinely concerned, which is laughable, given everything he's put me through.

"Are you telling me that, with your vampire hearing, you don't know what's just happened? Or last night either, for that matter?"

"I heard perfectly well. Which is why I didn't ask what

the issue was. I asked how you were feeling. I do realise that this situation might partly be down to me."

"Partly?"

Jesus, this guy is unbelievable. If this is an attempt at an apology, then it's a shit one.

"*All* of it is your fault. Everything was fine before you turned up. We were good, the three of us, Naz, Rey and I. We were doing okay."

"Apart from the fact that Rey had been thrown out of Blackwatch, Narissa was stealing information from you, and you were suffering from one of the most severe cases of unrequited love known to man."

"Fuck you, Calin."

A flash of regret crosses his face. "I'm sorry. I apologise. I know I messed things up for you. It may have escaped your notice, but I messed things up for myself, too."

"Yeah, well, you're not good enough for her, anyway."

"That's one thing we finally agree on."

He offers a conciliatory smile that I make no attempt to reciprocate.

"Perhaps I could talk to her. On your behalf, that is," he says. "Explain that you were only following my orders."

Kicking the floor, I take a deep breath. It makes it harder to hate the guy when he acts chivalrous, like this.

"Thanks, but I don't think that will help either of our cases. Besides, we'd have to find her first."

"You mean you don't know where she is?"

And just like that, I feel even worse.

13

Narissa

For the first few hours, nobody speaks. Esther is leading the way, followed by George, while Lou and I trail behind. Occasionally, I feel Lou gently nudging my block, trying to get me to speak to her, but I don't let her in. Her concern is palpable, and I know she only means well, but I've got nothing to say right now. Not to anybody. If I let her in, I'm not sure how much I'd be able to keep to myself, and that's not a risk I'm willing to take. So, we travel on, with me detached from the other three, the way I always wanted it back in the pack.

We keep the sun ahead of us as we move east. Where possible, we stick to woods and shadows, but it's mostly farmland. Cattle scatter as we approach, then a herd of sheep, and the dogs guarding them bark angrily at us. We always avoid anywhere people might see us.

By midday, we've been running non-stop for six hours when, as we approach a small copse, Esther comes to a halt and turns human. I don't know if she tried to talk to me as a wolf, but my only choice is to turn human too and listen to whatever it is she wants to say.

"Why have we stopped?" I ask immediately.

"I need to take a rest," she replies. "It's getting too hot."

"We'll be fine. There's a forest on the horizon. There'll be plenty of shade there."

"I need proper rest now. If I don't sleep, I'll start making mistakes and take us the wrong way."

"I thought you said you knew where to go?"

My words come out a little more harshly than I'd intended. While Lou looks concerned by my response, George and Esther observe me with disdain.

"I do know the way," Esther says, pointedly. "But my original scent has faded since I was last here and I have to concentrate if I'm not to miss it. Of course, if you want to go ahead without me, be my guest. We can catch you up. Or you can decide to become Alpha and I'd have to do whatever you say. I'd have to keep going."

My jaws clench at her remarks, but I'm not going to rise to the bait. I'm certainly not going to be bullied into taking on the role, which is what they keep trying to achieve. And saying I could go on ahead without her is stupid, and she knows it. So I don't bother to reply to either suggestion. A tense silence ensues, but true to form, Lou quickly breaks it.

"Do you not think we should have brought the rest of

the pack?" she says. "They've been asking where we are. Whenever we've done this before, we've gone as a whole pack."

"For starters, we're not a pack without an alpha, remember?" Esther looks pointedly at me as she says this. "We're just a bunch of lone wolves, guided by your mother."

"Esther said she thought there was only one vampire where we're heading." I redirect the conversation back to her. "Assuming she's correct, then the four of us will be more than enough to take it out."

"Provided I can actually get some rest first, that shouldn't be a problem," Esther replies.

Once again, the comment is aimed at me, and there's no point in further argument. It's abundantly clear that I wouldn't have a clue where to go. Besides, although I wasn't out on a run all night, like these guys were, I didn't exactly get a lot of sleep myself, either.

George remains silent and stoical. That's his go-to attitude. In fact, the entire time we've been together at Régine's, I don't think he's spoken more than a dozen sentences to me. There's no point wondering if he'd take my side and agree that we should keep moving. I may not know him well, but I'm smart enough to realise he'd follow Esther on anything. Poor guy. I think he must have a crush on her.

Knowing I've lost this battle, I turn back to wolf and head for the trees to find somewhere to lie down and rest. The second I close my eyes, the images start up. Oliver kissing me. Us so tight together it's as if we're moving as one. His lips against mine, then on my cheek, my neck, my shoulders, every part of me.

I love you, Naz. I've always loved you.

How many times did he say that to me last night? I lost count. And even though I couldn't bring myself to say the same to him, it still felt so good. But I don't know if I'll ever be able to look at him again, let alone speak to him.

At some point, while my emotions flickered between pity and anger, I must have fallen asleep, because the next thing I know, there's a weight pressing on me and Lou's shouting at my block. I let her in.

Naz, shall we go? The rest of us are ready, but we can stay here longer if you need more rest.

I squeeze my eyes shut, trying to remove the fog of sleep that's shrouding my thoughts. Lou is standing on me. Literally. Her front paws are pushing down on my shoulders. I blink and take stock of my surroundings. The sun is now on a downward descent, casting lengthy shadows beneath the trees. By the look of things, it won't be long until dusk. I guess I needed some sleep after all.

I'm good to go, I respond. *Just give me a second to stretch.*

I can sense George and Esther's impatience at the delay, but I take my time. As far as I'm concerned, the whole purpose of this trip is to stay away from Calin and Oliver and for as long as possible. Besides, they're the ones who wanted to stop in the first place. I don't take the piss though, and it's not long before I'm properly awake and ready.

The cooler air of the late afternoon helps us move quickly, and there's a small level of enjoyment to be had with all the unfamiliar sights and smells. On our previous missions, we travelled quite a distance. The first vampire nest we took out was near Munich. The second was in Austria, not far from Graz. This will be the first time we've ventured into Italy.

Once again, I keep my block up, but that means I'm left with my own thoughts, which of course keep wandering to things I'd rather not dwell on. So, I finally decide to open my mind up and let their chatter in.

Hey! Lou's voice is the first to come through. *We were just debating where exactly we are. George thinks we're still in France. I reckon we've already crossed into Germany. What do you think?*

We're going to Italy, Lou. I reply. *We don't need to go through Germany at all.*

Really are you sure?

I'm sure. Did you study any geography at school?

A hint of embarrassment comes through from her, and I feel my mood lighten. When I was her age, I was trawling bars, trying to find a vampire. Any sense of innocence I had was definitely lost early on. Seeing Lou like this, makes me wonder how I could have turned out, if there hadn't been so much darkness in my life.

So, Lou starts up again, obviously wanting to gloss over her glaring lack of geographical knowledge. *Why did you change your mind? I thought you said we weren't going to do any more vampire-killing trips. What happened?*

For the first time on this run, George's voice comes through.

You are joking, right? he laughs.

What?

Come on, Lou, Esther joins in. *Can't you tell? She and Oliver have had a lovers' tiff.*

What are you talking about? They're not lovers.

Don't worry, Lou, you'll recognise the scent well enough when you're older.

I feel for her. Despite all her many wolf talents, she remains remarkably naïve, and once again I sense a brief flash of embarrassment. This time, I'm the one who breaks the silence, to change the subject and help her out.

So, three days' travelling, that's what you said, right, Esther? That means we'll be gone less than a week?

That's the plan, she replies. *Are you sure you're going to cope with being away from your men for that long? There's always George, of course. Maybe he could become part of your little harem. What do you say, George?*

Not sure she could handle a wolf.

Oh, very funny. I'm glad you can get so much amusement at my expense, I say, giving in to the banter.

Oh, don't worry. We will. Tell me though, does that bust up mean Oliver is back on the market? Hunting always makes me frisky. Any objection to me jumping in when we get back? Of course, if you don't want that, you just have to say the word. The A word, that is.

I let out a growl to show my annoyance, but in truth, the banter is strangely cathartic. From what I've seen, wolves don't take themselves all that seriously in relationships. Perhaps I should take a leaf out of their book.

We continue running through the night, stopping the next morning to hunt and then sleep a little. I don't know if I'll ever get used to feeding like this. I don't like it at all. Feeling the life of an animal slip away as I crush it between

CHAPTER 13

my jaws is something I can't believe I will ever enjoy but needs must. The first time I had to do it was on that first mission, which I took charge of. That was a mistake. Ever since, there's been all this nonsense of me becoming Alpha. Right now, Esther's the one leading, and that's just how I like it.

We repeat the same routine the following day.

At around noon on the third day, Esther comes to a stop. We crossed over into Italy last night and have found ourselves on rolling hillsides covered in vineyards, with yellow-brick houses scattered amongst the fields. It looks more the type of destination someone would choose to go on honeymoon than hunt vampires.

Esther changes to human and the rest of us do likewise.

"It's not that much further," she says. "You'll be able to pick up the scent yourselves soon."

She walks over to the brow of the hill we're on and points across to the horizon.

"There."

I'm suddenly aware of a throbbing in the pit of my stomach. For the first time since we left, I wonder if this is a good idea.

14

We fall silent and, one by one, turn back to wolf. As we pick up on each other's feelings, there's a definite nervousness there. Even if we haven't yet caught the smell of vampire, we can feel something. There's a change in the air, like a storm's brewing. But there are no clouds above us, just a clear blue sky. We walk on slowly, every footstep carefully considered as we fine tune our senses.

The other missions didn't feel like this. They had an almost party atmosphere. We knew, with our numbers, we could take on even a hundred vampires. There was never any doubt. But in this small group, we're feeling quite apprehensive.

There's no tree cover now. We're passing through open vineyards, where rows of plants are bowing under the weight of grapes. The aroma of the fruit is heady, blocking out all others. Until that single one hits us, and Lou's voice comes through.

That's it! Do you guys smell it, too? It's definitely vampire, isn't it? I'm sure it is.

It's faint. Barely a hint, carried on the slightest of breezes, but it's present. It's not accompanied by quite the same level of death and decay that we found at the other nests, but it's vampire all right. Then, as quickly as it appeared, it's gone again.

I've lost it, I tell the others. *Anyone else still got it?*

Silence. Maybe we were wrong. Perhaps this whole thing is a mistake, and we should head back and return later with the others. I keep this thought to myself and instead try to lighten the mood with conversation.

When did you find this place, Esther? I ask, openly. *You're sure there's only one vampire here?*

Positive. Only one scent in the whole area. That was it. Nothing but this dude. No animals. Not even any humans.

This doesn't make me feel any better. I try more questions, to get as much information as I can before we face this thing. Not to mention to keep us all distracted from what might come next.

How long ago was that?

Just after the pack broke up. I stayed here a while and caught the scent many times.

I now realise I know nothing of what happened to her after Juliette attacked my mother's pack. Chrissie and Lou stuck together; that much I do know. As for the other wolves, well let's just say I've been holding off from bonding. But now we're here like this, it seems silly not to ask.

How did you end up here? How long was it until you found the others?

A flash of pain comes through from her. It was a distressing time for everyone, but this is acute. It feels like it's my own heart breaking.

It's okay, I say, quickly backtracking. *You don't need to tell me. I'm sorry. I shouldn't have asked.*

It's fine. It's fine.

Despite her words, she pauses, and for a second, I think she's not going to speak again, but after a moment, she takes a deep breath and starts.

I was there when the vampires came to the pack. I don't know if you were aware, but I wasn't one of those who ran into the forest with you, to cover your tracks. I stayed behind to meet Juliette. To help protect her, as I thought.

More pain runs through her, this time accompanied by a surge of anger.

Your mother wanted to help her; you know that. She thought she'd been kidnapped by the vampires on her way to us. She thought they were holding her hostage. We all did. Why else would a wolf be in their company? By the time she realised—we all realised—they were working together, it was too late.

Her thoughts stop for a moment, but her feelings do not. Nor do ours. Collective grief grasps us as Esther continues.

The few of us who were able to resist Juliette's commands as the new Alpha, either ran or fought. My brother and mother brought down a vampire, before wolves from our own pack turned on them. It was then we realised all was lost. The last thing they did was to scream at us to go. Begged my wife and me to get to safety. So that's what we did. I was in the lead as we ran through the forest away from the screaming and the mayhem. I ran, and I ran, and I didn't look back ... until it was too late.

There's another pause and I want to offer her my sympathy, but it's Lou's voice that comes through.

I remember. Ruth always loved Italy. Her thoughts are full of compassion and it's not hard to tell from the swell of emotion that they're talking about Esther's wife.

I thought she was behind me, she continues. *Our Alpha was dead, so I was able to put up a block and keep my thoughts sealed off from all the havoc. When I finally opened up to the pack again, all the voices were gone ... including Ruth's.*

It seems disrespectful, walking casually beside her as she shares this harrowing story. I feel we should stop and give her the chance to breathe. But she's the one leading us, so I just listen as she continues.

Ruth always wanted to visit Italy, dreamed about coming here for years. She'd talked about it since she was a child, mainly because of how much she loved pizza, I think.

We would have definitely got along, I say, only to immediately regret it. What a crass comment to make. She's talking about her dead wife and I'm talking about food. But a flicker of appreciation and a sad smile transfer from her to me and I feel slightly less stupid.

When we got married, Freya and the pack surprised us with two plane tickets here. That was something about your mother. She always did the unexpected. Always went that little bit further to make sure her pack was happy. Her only instruction was that we had to stay human for the two weeks of the honeymoon, so that no vampires would become aware we were travelling. But that wasn't hard at all. Two weeks of newly wedded bliss. It was perfect. We spent our days like normal people, lazing on the beaches, taking wine-tasting tours of the vineyards with other couples. It was fun, an escape, but we did start to miss the pack after a while. If we ever decide we've had enough of the wolf life, this is where we should come, she said. Return to Italy and live out our days eating bruschetta, sitting on our veranda.

So, this was where I had to come. I ran day and night without stopping to reach here as quickly as I could. I knew, if she'd escaped, this was where she would head. I was completely reckless, crossing towns, even cities, as a wolf. I was spotted a few times but luckily not by anyone who understood what they had seen. And there was no one in my head to reprimand me. No alpha commanding me to return to the pack.

I reached the village where we'd stayed all those years ago and hid in a nearby stand of trees. For days and nights, I waited, refusing to turn back to human or even fall asleep for fear I might miss her calling to me. I began to hear things. Lack of sleep does that. It creates illusions, as does starvation. Two weeks passed, and then George found me. I was very weak and not in a great place, mentally. I'm not sure I would have survived much longer. George made me eat, helped me get my strength back. He also had to be the one to tell me my Ruth was gone.

In that moment, the feeling of love and respect exchanged between the two of them is almost overwhelming. I don't know what their relationship was before all this. Friends? Acquaintances? Maybe they were always close, but I know that now it's something deeper. A shared pain.

All that flirting with Oliver to wind me up, the bravado. I realise now it was just a way of disguising what she was really feeling. And I can't blame her. I'm not so different. Not really.

CHAPTER 14

We reach the crest of a large hill, and she comes to a stop.

There, can you smell it? It's on the wind now. We're close.

Lifting my nose, I take in a deep lungful of fresh air but find it tainted with that unforgettable sour tang. It's more than a hint now, it's overwhelming.

It's probably time to get ready.

15

The view from the top of the hill shows us just how expansive this countryside is. Into the distance, roll endless, yellow-brown hills—some with vineyards or smallholdings—and a number of villages, separated by miles of farmland. Some are just a cluster of five or six buildings in the bottom of a valley, while others are larger with church spires that pierce the sky. The setting sun is just a sliver on the horizon now, painting everything in pinky-orange hues.

As I gaze out, I think about the training Oliver had me do when we were on the run, the hill sprints, in particular. I'm glad we weren't in a place like this; I can't imagine the torturous exercises he'd have devised for me. Thoughts of Oliver and earlier times spent together, lead to a dull ache in my chest.

It will soon be dark, George says, drawing my attention away from the view. *Even if it is only one vampire, I don't think we should risk attacking by night.*

I could definitely do with some sleep, Lou adds, stretching out her legs.

We're all in agreement that, in an unplanned situation like this, striking before daylight would be a bad idea. So, this means we need to find somewhere to hunker down. However, before I can even think about sleeping arrangements, I need water and the others agree.

Running for so long on rough terrain, would be hard for anyone, but when you're a wolf, encased in inches of thick fur, it doesn't take long to start overheating, and in the sun, it can be a killer. The first farmhouse we come to, we change into human form and grab some clothes from a washing line.

"I always thought Italy would be greener than this, didn't you?" Lou says, when we're a safe distance away, demonstrating her inability to stay silent for long. "It's always green in the pictures you see, isn't it?"

"It's green in springtime," Esther says, keeping her eyes fixed ahead. "It was when Ruth and I were here."

Goats with bells around their necks watch us pass from higher ground, although there are no signs of anyone tending them. In fact, other than the occasional distant growl of a car engine, there's hardly any evidence of people at all.

"We should head to that village," George says, pointing. "Large ones often have fountains in their centre."

"Okay," I say, "but no changing into wolves from now on, guys. We should stay human. The wind direction is in our favour at the moment, but if it changes, we don't want the vampire to realise we're around. Especially as we can't attack until morning. We'll have to do the rest of this on foot."

Esther looks at me, with what borders on a smile.

"Sounds like something a good alpha would say," she comments.

I ignore her and keep walking.

Stealing clothes is pretty easy as long as you can choose when you change. There have only been a couple of times in the last few months when I've not been able to find a washing line with a dress or baggy T-shirt hanging on it, ready and waiting.

Shoes, on the other hand are a different matter. You hardly ever come across them, and if you do, you'll be lucky if they're anywhere near the right size. As a result, my feet are now a podiatrist's nightmare, with calloused soles as hard as leather, usually capable of dealing with the most unforgiving of surfaces. But the ground here is very rough, covered with rocks and sharp stones and there are brambles everywhere, too. This part of our journey—even for the others who are more used to it—is torturously slow.

We pick our way the best we can, our sights set on reaching the village by nightfall, but it takes longer than we expected. By the time we finally clamber up the steps to the small piazza, the sky is littered with stars.

"I'm parched," Lou says, echoing what most of us must be thinking. "Where did you say the fountain would be?"

"If there is one, somewhere near here," George comments, looking around. "Maybe this way."

No one has a better idea or the energy to disagree, so we silently follow him. It proves to be the right decision. As

CHAPTER 15

we turn a corner, there it is. A brass pipe juts out over a stone bowl, and above it is a metal disc, polished smooth with use.

I step back and let the others go first, starting with Lou. She pushes the button and water trickles out.

"This place feels odd," George says to me as we wait for our turn.

"Well, that vampire smell was pretty entrenched. There's a good chance no one ventures out at night."

"Maybe, but this is Europe. People generally stay up late. Something doesn't feel right."

It's hard to disagree. I look up at the buildings, searching for any sign of life. As I look more closely, I can see many of them have large cracks in their walls and it seems that they may, in fact, be uninhabited.

"I'm not sure the lack of people has anything to do with the vampires," I say pointing to the damage.

"Earthquake, perhaps," George reflects. "They're not uncommon in Italy. It would explain why there's no one living here. Better to build somewhere else that seems safe than try to make repairs only to have it happen again."

That seems a good theory, but something else doesn't seem to gel.

"Why would a vampire choose to live where there aren't people? It has to feed."

"Maybe it's got a personal supply."

I shudder at this idea, my mind returning to that night at the Blood Bank, where people offered themselves up in the hope of being turned themselves. It was bad enough then, but it's worse now I know the truth—that none of the vampires there had the lower fangs necessary to turn people. They were just using them as their playthings, pure and simple.

Trying to erase the image of humans on leashes, I return to the moment. It's possible this vampire has gone down that route, got himself a little acolyte. But then Esther said she'd detected only one scent. Maybe it travels to a different area for food. It would certainly have enabled it to go undetected here more easily.

When Esther, Lou and George have had their fill at the waterspout, I take my turn. The first sip makes me realise just how thirsty I am. The cool liquid runs down my chin as eagerly bring it to my mouth.

"Is anyone else hungry?" Lou asks, as I step back. "Because I'm starving, and I think we passed some fruit trees in a garden on our way in. If we're going to fight tomorrow, I definitely need to eat something. I mean, we could turn and hunt, but you said we shouldn't, Naz. Shall I see what I can find?"

"Sounds good. I'll come with you," Esther says.

"We might as well all go," I add, seeing no point in me and George waiting here.

We follow Lou back and find she was correct. Even before we push open the gate—if you can call it that, the way it's hanging off its hinges—we see fruit littering the ground.

This house is also abandoned. The windows are broken, two of them having no glass left at all, and the front door stands ajar and covered in a thick mesh of cobwebs. For now, though, we focus on the garden.

Apple and pear trees, which look as if they haven't been pruned or maintained in any way for years, have grown with intertwined branches. My bare feet detect a path beneath the knee-high grass. There are brambles too, sporting blackberries which offer that wonderful sour tang, and bushes covered in small red berries that could well be red currents, but I'm not going to risk eating something I don't recognise. Apples and blackberries will do for me.

We continue to pick the fruit. Despite the lack of illumination, the moonlight makes it easy enough to see what we're doing. We chatter light-heartedly about mindless things, like how old Régine might be, what she has on Henri and how much the others in the pack would have loved her place.

Eventually a lull in conversation allows a wave of tiredness to sweep through us. It's accompanied by a mixture of anticipation and apprehension, like the night before the first day at a new school.

"We should sleep," I say, feeling one of us needs to say it. "There's probably somewhere in the house suitable to camp down. I'll keep first watch and I'll yell if there's any hint of trouble."

Esther nods. It's a sign of how tired we all are that no one disagrees. Normally, people jump over each other for the first shift, but there's none of that now.

"Wake me up to take over," George says, as they head inside, and I tell him I will.

And then it's just me. Me and my thoughts. Exactly what I've been trying to avoid.

For a while, I amble around the garden, with no real

purpose, just to kill time. If I was back at the Chateau, I'd lose myself in a book. Régine's got a fair number of English texts. If there were ever any books in this house, I'm sure they'd be in French even if the damp or silverfish hadn't already got to them.

My thoughts drift back to my friends. Friends. That feels like the wrong term to use. There's Rey, who hates me so much she wants to destroy me, Oliver, who's been lying to my face for months and Calin. Calin … were we ever even friends? I think we were just infatuated with each other for a while.

I feel a pang of guilt about how I've treated him. Or rather, how I've treated him in comparison to Oliver. I realise I've been blaming him for what happened to my mother. That's something I haven't been willing to admit to myself until now. It's not just that I'm angry at him for not telling me she had died, I actually blame him for her death. He promised me he'd keep her safe.

But what are promises? Just words that dissolve into the air the moment they're spoken. Well, I won't make that mistake again. I won't give any more promises. Nor will I expect them.

After another hour, my eyelids become itchy and heavy, and I know there's no point trying to carry on like this. Carefully, so as not to wake Esther or Lou, I tiptoe through the house and shake George by the shoulder.

I'm half asleep before my head touches the floor.

16

The dawn chorus has come and gone by the time I open my eyes the next morning. Light floods in through the broken windows, casting criss-cross shadows on the floor. The room is empty.

I find the others outside, tucking into a breakfast of more fruit.

"You slept well," Lou says, handing me a pear.

"I must have needed it."

"I think we all did."

The pear is ridiculously sweet. As soon as it's finished, I head over to the tree and pull off a second one, although my eyes are bigger than my belly and I struggle to finish it. Maybe it's because of how much we ate last night. Then again, perhaps it's nerves about what's coming next.

I can feel all eyes on me, waiting for instructions. Part of me wants to ignore it and let someone else make the decisions. But the sky is mostly clear, and apart from some ominous black shapes to the north, the sun is burning brightly. The last thing I want is for it to cloud over because we've procrastinated.

"I guess it's time we do this, then," I say.

Lou's face cracks into a wide smile.

"Great, I've been ready since dawn."

Her usual eagerness is endearing, but this time, it worries me. Normally, Chrissie, her mother, is with us. The fact she's not means Lou's my responsibility. Technically, as it was my idea to come here, they should all be my responsibility, but that's alpha thinking, and the other two are old enough to make their own bad decisions.

"No theatrics," I say, as we strip off our clothes and prepare to change. "Just in and out. Even if it is just one there, no stupid risks."

There's no need to worry about the vampire catching our scent now. Even if it does realise we're coming, it's trapped inside by daylight.

"*No theatrics,*" Esther mimics my voice. "You know you sound more and more like an alpha every day."

"Well, I might sound like one, but I'm not one. If anyone else wants to give out instructions, feel free."

My voice sounds stern, commanding, in a way I hadn't anticipated, and there's a definite smirk on her face. Well, she can grin all she likes. Making sure a mission is well run is not the same as wanting to lead a pack, and after today, we're going to have to stick to what I said and cut back on these trips. The last thing we need is Juliette finding out what we're up to and putting Adam at risk.

"Let's do this then. Let's go kill the vampire," Lou says before diving into her wolf form.

There's no holding back now. It's easy to tell from the lack of scent that people haven't lived here for a long time, so we don't have to worry about anyone seeing us. We sprint through the village, past faded shop signs and empty windows, over a crumbling bridge and down the side of a hill into the farmland beyond, following the scent we caught onto yesterday.

It doesn't take long before it's almost thick in the air. There's something about the smell of a vampire that's overpowering to wolves, and it soon becomes the only thing we're aware of. Without needing to communicate, we slow down.

It's close. Lou speaks first. *But there's just a farmhouse. It wouldn't be somewhere like that would it?*

Previously, our search for nests has led us to desolate places: forests in Lithuania and Austria, a rundown apartment block in Munich, all in darkness or deep shadow even during daylight hours, giving them the ability to move around freely. Somewhere like where we stayed last night would have fitted the bill nicely, but the house we're approaching is quite different. Flowers are thriving in the sunny garden. Admittedly wildflowers, rather than ones that have been cultivated, but flowers none the less. If it wasn't for the smell, I'd be certain we'd got this wrong.

A waist-height wall runs around the building, which is pretty basic and can't comprise more than three or four rooms. It's whitewashed, but the paint is old and flaking in places, and the wrought-iron gate that opens onto a paved path has rusted. I slowly pad around the wall, which I could easily jump, but don't. My hackles are up. Something is wrong. This isn't the type of place a vampire would use.

Esther, is this what it was like before? I ask.

I didn't get this close. All I got was the smell, from a distance.

Maybe it's been made to look nice as a way of trapping people, Lou suggests. *You know, like Hansel and Gretel with the witch and her house made of sweets. Maybe the vampire's based this place on that.*

Or maybe the Hansel and Gretel witch was based on this vampire, I think but keep to myself.

Let's get this done, George says.

It's not surprising he's touchy. He took almost the whole of the night shift after me, only waking Lou an hour or so before dawn. I can feel his impatience to get started.

Something doesn't feel right, I comment, unable to distract myself from a churning in my gut.

It's a vampire nest. Nothing about it is right, Esther counters. *Now are we standing here deliberating all day, or are we going in?*

There's no logical reason I can offer them to delay any further. If they want to carry on, what right do I have to stop them, just because I have a bad feeling in my stomach? But I can't help myself.

We should wait.

Shouldn't we make the most of the clear skies? Lou asks. *Those black clouds are coming nearer.*

And fast, Esther adds.

They're both right. It hasn't escaped me, but I can't give the word to go. Something won't let me.

I tell you what. I'll get this started, George says. *I don't mind leading the pack for this one.* And without waiting for any of us to respond, he shifts his weight to his back legs, preparing to spring up and over the wall.

I watch his muscles tense and flex. As he moves, one of the clouds passes across the sun. And in that split second, I notice something shimmer above the brickwork. A trip wire! I see it too late to prevent him from leaping straight into the trap.

STOP! I shriek, but to no avail. As he registers my panic, his paw hits the cable, and a spike flashes towards him. A second later, a searing pain is felt by us all as he drops to the ground, yelping.

George! Esther screams and moves to follow him.

Don't! I shout. *You mustn't go after him!*

I'm about to lunge to pin her down and stop her, when the sun reappears and a figure steps out of the house and renders us both frozen to the spot.

That's a vampire, Lou whispers, *and it's standing in broad daylight.*

17

I've seen Calin out in the sun before, collar up, cap and gloves on. He generally only goes out like that on overcast days or in the evening, and while not in enormous discomfort, he always gives the impression he'd rather not be there. But this vampire is wearing only cotton shorts with sandals on his feet. Nothing on his legs. Nothing on his chest and arms at all. No hat. It would be perfectly possible to believe he wasn't a vampire at all, if it were not for his fangs—top and bottom—which glisten in the sunlight as he stares at us.

George? George? Esther's voice continues to yell in our heads. *Please, please be okay! George, speak to me! George!*

The seconds tick by, and I feel my heart rising into my throat, enough to choke me. Time seems to stand still. Then, weakly, we hear his voice crackle in our minds.

I'm here. I'm still with you.

Thank God.

He's in severe pain. His anguish is flowing through us

all. I can't tell exactly where he's hurt. Around the chest area would be my guess, basically, the worst place possible. Please don't let it be an organ. If it's pierced something like a lung and we can't get it out to enable him to start healing, the results will be catastrophic. I keep my thoughts of what could be blocked from the others, but I know they're thinking the same thing. Stepping back, I try to see if there's a way to get over the wall to him without triggering another trap. As I move away, I stare at the vampire. He's angry. That much is certain, and he's saying something to us. My stomach knots. The lump in my throat is now making me gag. If I turn human to understand what he's saying, I'd be at my most vulnerable. Besides, why should I? I haven't listened to any others of his kind before I killed them. But none of them were on their own. And none of them had flowers in their gardens, either.

Before I have a chance to decide what to do, something else catches my eye. Esther.

Just like me, she saw the trip wire. Saw where George's foot caught and triggered the release of whatever it was that struck him. She springs forwards, high into the air. Higher than I've ever seen a wolf leap before. She's across the wall and into the garden, jaws snapping, teeth bared, ready to sink them into the vampire's neck. One on one, a wolf always wins, even indoors, where there's no sunlight to weaken the vampire. Yet as she flies towards him, he steps aside, clenches his fist and, using her momentum against her, strikes her across the muzzle, sending her flying into the wall of the house.

I gasp as she cries out, hits the wall and lands on the

ground with a thud. The vampire just batted a fully grown wolf aside like he was swatting a fly. Fear flashes through Lou. I try to keep mine hidden, but I don't even know if that's possible.

That bastard is mine!

Esther is on her feet, ready to go again. Her pain is minimal, compared to George's, at least.

Esther no. Not again. You don't know what he's capable of.

She's growling and snapping, but the vampire looks only mildly irritated. Certainly not fearful.

Stay where you are! I say to the others as she prepares to attack again. *We're doing this my way, now. If anything happens to me, you run. Get it? You get George, run and don't stop.*

That thing needs to die, Esther barks back. I can feel the torment as she pads up and down, crying out to George. All the time I've known her, she's only ever been cool, calm and collected, even yesterday, when she told us about Ruth. But not now. Now, she can barely steady her thoughts, and I suspect it's only fear of the unknown that's stopped her from lunging at him again, already. But soon, her need to get to George will overcome that.

We need to kill that bastard now. George is bleeding. I can smell his blood.

He's bleeding as a wolf, I counter. *He's got time to heal if he doesn't get attacked again. I need to talk to this vampire.*

You can't be serious!

She's fighting me. Any moment now, she's going to attack for a second time. But he defended himself with such ease. It wasn't even a fight. If it had been, I know who'd have been the winner. There's only one way I can get her to do what I tell her and stop her from getting herself killed. And as much as I don't want this, I want to see a new friend die even less.

This is an order, Esther! An order from your Alpha!
You're ...
I'm taking my place as Alpha. Now back down.
You ... you ...

She can't object. She's been burning for this for so long, for the sake of the pack. My words have caused something to shift. I can feel it, not only inside me but also around me, as if the whole universe has witnessed what I've just said and agreed. I'm ninety-five percent certain that this is a truly terrible decision, but right now it's the only way I can think of keeping Esther and Lou safe and hopefully getting to George, before it's too late.

You all stay as wolves. And if anything happens to me, you run.

They can't refuse me now. Not anymore, even though I feel their anguish. The vampire is still standing there in broad daylight, watching us. I must change. I have to do this.

Closing my eyes, I take a deep breath. When I open them again, I'm on two legs, my toes on the cold, damp grass. Now that I'm standing here, human, I'm not sure what to say, but he starts to speak.

"I made a vow, many years ago, not to kill any of your kind, but tell Polidori that if he sends you again, I will break it."

"Polidori?"

Of all the things I'd though he might say, mentioning the vampire who leads the Council and wants me dead, was not one of them. I feel the warmth drain from my skin.

"You know Polidori?"

"Not through choice."

His voice is gruff. Raspy, like you'd expect of an old man, but he doesn't look like that. He looks even younger than me, in fact, although I know more than enough not to be deceived by appearances. He knows Polidori. And he's a vampire who still has his bottom fangs.

A memory triggers in the back of my mind. One of Calin and me in the cabin together at the wolf pack. If he knows of Polidori and still has his bottom fangs he must be either newly turned or very old. Judging by his ability to stay out in the sunlight for so long, I'm guessing the latter.

As I'm contemplating what to do next, he comes across to the wall, where George is lying on the ground, still whimpering. Esther was right about the blood, it's pooling beneath him, silvery red, glistening in the sunlight. His eyes are bright with fear as the vampire hovers over him, but it could be worse. They could be registering nothing at all.

Esther and Lou growl.

"Get away from him," I say, pushing open the gate and stepping into the garden. I can change fast if I need to. But faster than he can kill George? I'd rather not have to find out.

"Wow, you really are paranoid, aren't you?"

He sighs, as if our presence is boring him. Like we're no threat to him at all.

"I'm just going to get this out of his shoulder. You can do it yourself, if you'd prefer."

He steps back, waiting for me to accept or decline.

"What did you hit him with? Was it silver? Ash wood?"

"Wood, yes. But not ash. Pine. Take it out yourself, if you'd rather," he offers again.

I don't feel I've got a choice. If this vampire takes one step closer to George, he could end his life in a second. Then again, one step closer to me and that could be my fate. My gut's telling me to do it. Unfortunately, I can't think of a time when my instincts have ever served me particularly well. Still, I drop to George's side. Blood has stained his fur almost black and there's about an inch of wood still sticking out of him. I grab the end in my fingers.

"This will only hurt for a second," I say, praying I'm right and don't screw it up. I don't exactly have much experience when it comes to this type of thing. Adjusting my fingers to get the best possible grip, I grit my teeth and yank upwards with all my might.

George's howl pierces the air, and Esther leaps towards him. I don't stop her. I'm too fixated on what I've got in my hand. It's a perfectly smooth piece of wood, sanded along the edges and sharpened to a point at one end. I'm holding a stake. The implication of what this means takes less than a second to form in my mind.

"This is for killing vampires," I say.

"You catch on quick."

"But you're a vampire."

He snorts. Not in a derogatory way. More like he's amused.

"Wow, this pack has got a bright one as their alpha."

It's the first time I've heard that term used in relation to me. Alpha. His comment was obviously not meant as a compliment, and yet I'm filled with more pride than I would have expected. But I can't dwell on that right now.

"Why would you want to kill vampires? Are you working for Polidori?"

His eyes narrow on me.

"He's really not sent you to get me?"

"Trust me, Polidori and I are not on the best of terms."

"Then we have something in common."

He hesitates for a moment or two, then nods towards the other wolves.

"Perhaps you should come inside. I have some tea. It will help him with the shock. Not that you wolves need much help, but it'll speed things along. And I think maybe we need to talk."

18

I don't trust him, Esther's says immediately when I change back and tell the others what he's said. *He's a vampire.*

Calin's a vampire, Lou counters. *Being a vampire isn't synonymous with being untrustworthy.*

No, just out of all the vampires we've met, we know only one good one. The odds aren't exactly favourable.

Or maybe they are. I mean, the fact we've met so many bad ones, means we're probably due to meet another good one, doesn't it?

This argument has the potential to go back and forth for hours. Thankfully, I now have the authority to stop it.

Look, I want to hear him out. That trap wasn't set for us. It was set with stakes. Stakes to strike at chest level. He was trying to stop other vampires coming in. You know what they say. The enemy of my enemy is my friend.

Or the enemy of my enemy is just another enemy, Esther replies, sarcastically.

This isn't up for discussion, this isn't a democracy anymore, I say, finally using what I guess I can call my Alpha voice. *You wanted me to be in charge, so here I am. And I want to hear what he has to say.*

I turn around, ready to give them the order to change into human form and realise he's no longer in the garden.

Where did he go?

It's George who answers. Since removing the stake, his wound has been healing. The bleeding stopped almost immediately, though I expect it will be sore to run on for a little while.

He went into the house. You can hear him banging around in there. Sounds like he's put the kettle on.

Making tea. That was what he said.

Look, I know you're not sure about this, but I have a feeling. After we've heard him out, if we don't like what he says, then we can kill him, together, as a pack. Or leave him be. But for now, I want you all human. Do you think you can manage that, George?

I feel his agreement. *Just don't ask me to throw a javelin any time soon, and I should be fine.*

Great. Human it is.

Of all the weirdness I've encountered since being a werewolf and before that too, this has to be the weirdest. People following my instructions or rather, having to follow my instructions. I'm all about free will and everything, but this feeling is insane; no wonder some alphas, like Juliette, can get power crazy. I imagine it's hard to give something like this up. If you wanted it in the first place, that is. I'll be more than happy to let it go once I know we're all safe.

As we morph back, the vampire comes to the doorway.

"I've made tea, if you'd like to come inside. Or we could drink it out here, if you'd feel safer? I'll just need to get something to cover up in. I think I've probably exceeded my recommended daily dose of vitamin D."

The others' eyes turn to me and await my answer. I've already pointed out that this is no longer a democracy, so I guess this is on me, too.

"Out here will be better for us," I say, feeling I've already pushed these guys enough.

"Fine, there's a table around the back. I'll need to fetch a couple more chairs."

He points to a narrow path leading between the garden wall and the side of the house.

"I promise there are no more trip wires, but you can wait for me, if you'd rather."

"We'll wait," George says.

I nod, allowing his comment.

"We'll wait."

He disappears into the house.

"I don't get it. Why's he being so nice?" Lou whispers. "I mean, he's being really nice."

"A moment ago, you were the one who said not all vampires were evil," Esther replies.

"Yes, but there's evil and then there's nice. Calin's not evil, but he's never offered to make me tea."

"You do know that he has vampire hearing, don't you?" I say, feeling that the job of Alpha may involve far more mollycoddling than I would ever have imagined. "He can hear everything you're saying."

"You should listen to your Alpha," he says from the doorway. "Although I admit it's quite amusing, I haven't been spoken about with such interest in quite some time.

I'm not sure I've been called nice by a wolf in a while, either. Here, I thought you could use these. I'm afraid I go more for practicality and comfort than anything else."

He hands me a pile of clothes.

"Of course, if you want to stay as nature intended, that's fine. But the wolves I knew always preferred to be dressed when in human form."

"You knew other wolves?" I ask.

"I did. A very long time ago. And like I said, I made a vow to protect your kind. It was the least I could do …"

His gaze drifts momentarily away, like he's returning somewhere in his memory that he hasn't been to for a very long time. The way his forehead creases makes me think it's not a pleasant place to go.

"I'm Narissa," I say, stretching out my hand while Lou takes the clothes from me.

"Please to meet you, Narissa. I'm Rhett."

Lou yelps, and I turn to see she's dropped everything on the ground. Her skin is ashen, completely white, and she's not the only one. Esther and George look as if they've seen a ghost. They're frozen to the spot, and it's so quiet, I can hear the wind rustling through the trees around us.

It's Lou who finds her voice first.

"Rhett, as in the vampire who saved Eve? The one she called the Father of Wolves?"

He presses his lips together, then sighs.

"That would be me."

19

Sitting sipping tea with a vampire older than werewolves, was not how I had expected the morning to pan out. Particularly not with Lou, George and Esther fan-girling away beside me. Maybe it's a sign that I need to know a bit more about my heritage.

"You're the reason Eve survived," Lou says again.

"Possibly."

"You were there when werewolves were first created."

"I was."

"So, you're old. Really old."

"I am."

That would probably explain his ability to withstand sunlight. He's had centuries to build up some kind of resistance. Who knows what else he'd be capable of doing?

"Tell us about Eve," Esther's asking now. "She was sixteen when she was turned, wasn't she? And how was it that none of the others who were captured and experimented on at the same time as she was didn't survive? We have the Book of Eve, but it's old. Pages are missing, others faded. We've pieced the story together as best we can, but maybe, if we get the chance, we could go through it all with you. You could tell us everything you remember. It would be such a blessing to us."

Whether they're blind to his unease or simply too overwhelmed to care, I'm not sure, but it's obvious from where I'm sitting that this conversation is making Rhett more than a tad uncomfortable. I could use my alpha authority to stop them pestering him, but that would seem a bit unfair, particularly as I've got questions I want answered, too.

"I'm sure there'll be time for Rhett to tell us more, later," I say, my interruption gaining me a look of appreciation from the ancient vampire but one of annoyance from the others. I ignore that and focus back on what is more urgent right now. We have other, more pressing, things we need to discuss.

"You thought Polidori had sent us," I say. "Why?"

He looks away from me and picks up the teapot to refill our mismatched cups.

"I heard he had wolves working for him. I assumed you were with them."

"How did you find that out? Did you speak to him?"

He snorts again.

"I haven't seen him in over *two hundred years*, since he came here and asked me to be on that Council of his. Since I refused, we've given each other a wide berth."

"Why?"

He raises an eyebrow.

"Why what? Why didn't I join him, or why did we give each other a wide berth?"

"Both, I suppose."

He sips his tea, considering his answer.

"I'm not a people person. Or rather, I should say, I'm not a vampire person. I don't need something like the Blood Pact to tell me that devouring humans is not a good thing to do. It's basic decency, part of a moral compass we're all born with that shouldn't go away just because we happen to die. Too many of my kind have forgotten that. They think their power and their urges give them carte blanche to behave however they choose. Polidori respected my decision. Or at least he said he did. But I think he felt it would have helped his cause to have me on side."

"Why?"

"Because he's Rhett!" Lou says, with exasperation.

"As you've seen, being an old vampire like myself has its advantages. I'm stronger and far more resistant to sunlight, too. My senses have also become heightened. But it's more than that. There's a level of respect afforded us, partly to do with how long we've existed but mostly because of our power."

I recall what Calin said to me about Polidori and the respect he's given because of his age. Being that old means you've survived everything life, and death, has thrown at you. The witches, the purges, the vampire hunts. Dead or not, it's still a case of survival of the fittest. And Rhett's a vampire who's literally the stuff of legend; it's no wonder Polidori wanted him.

"But if peace is so important to you, then surely joining

the Council would have been the best way to achieve it?" I say. "The Council is there to help keep the peace, after all."

"Polidori was always ambitious, even before he was turned. Status is the most important thing to him. I guess I suspected that, eventually, something like this would happen."

His words trigger a tension in me.

"Something like what? What do you know is coming?"

His eyes return to his teacup, but he doesn't lift it. He just stares at it for a moment before speaking again. This time, his words are directed at me.

"I said I hadn't seen Polidori for over two hundred years, and that's true to a point. We went all that time with barely a letter exchanged. Then, two months ago, he turned up here again."

Goosebumps prickle on my skin. We're sitting in the same place where Polidori had been only a few months before, and it doesn't feel good.

"What did you talk about?"

"I didn't talk. I listened. He said there was a change coming. One that would elevate vampires to their rightful place in world hierarchy. He hoped that I would join him this time. Or, at least, respect his actions."

"What did you say?"

"As long as he left my corner of the world alone, I didn't care what he did."

For someone who appears infinitely powerful, this response feels almost like cowardice, looking after number one and damn what happens to the rest of us. My level of respect for Rhett drops.

"So, then what?" I ask. "What did he do?"

"He seemed relatively happy with my answer, or at least he pretended he was, but I've never trusted the man. Hence the traps. I assume you know what he's up to."

I shake my head.

"No. We have other wolves—undercover in a big pack he's got at his beck and call—feeding us information. But they take their orders from their alpha, who's part of his hierarchy, and have no idea why they're being asked to carry out the things they're doing. He's building up vampire numbers, we know that much, and leaving them with both sets of fangs. And, just as worrying, he's had a couple of witches fighting for him, too."

I expect this to elicit a response from him, a raised eyebrow at least. After all, witches hate vampires even more than wolves do, but there's nothing. He's completely impassive.

"But you're a pack," he says. "Why don't you take over this one that's helping him? Is that not a possibility? Whatever the number of vampires, if all you wolves band together, you'd be able to make quick work of them."

It all sounds so simple. Take back Juliette's pack. Turn on Polidori. I don't know where to begin with the list of reasons that make it so much harder than he could imagine. Before I can answer, Lou is talking. Rambling Lou.

"The Alpha of the other wolf pack is really horrid, like crazily sadistic. She killed Freya, our last Alpha, who was Naz's mum, only she didn't. She got someone else to do it with a gun, which is completely against wolf code. Most of our pack went with her, because she threatened to kill them if they didn't and only a few of us got away and none of us were really alpha material. And then there's the thing with one of the witches Naz, mentioned. She's Naz's best friend. Or at least she was. She did all this dark magic for Polidori, and now it's kind of consumed her, so Naz doesn't want to do anything until she's better. And the only one that can really lead us is Naz, although she really doesn't want to be our Alpha. So you see, until this stuff with Rey, that's the witch who's her friend, is sorted, we can't really do much at all."

If I'd been planning on keeping our cards close to my chest, Lou would have well and truly scuppered that, as she's just laid out pretty much everything. Both Esther and George are wide eyed in shock at her outburst. Rhett is quiet. Contemplative.

"You will need to find a witch to help your friend. Only she would be able to bring her back to the light."

"That would be great," I say, finally getting a word in. "Any idea where?"

Given how long Rey searched for another like herself, it's a flippant thing to say, but Rhett's response isn't.

"As a matter of fact, yes. I do."

20

This could still be a trap.

George is trailing behind a little due to his limp, but he's definitely healing quicker now in wolf form.

It's almost certainly a trap, Esther agrees.

It's night-time, you do realise that? It's night-time, and he's walking us into the middle of nowhere, where there's bound to be a vampire nest. We're all going to die.

You were the one who told him about Rey, Lou. In fact, you told him almost everything. I'm surprised you didn't give him our telephone number and a WhatsApp pin to Régine, too.

You're the Alpha. Why didn't you stop me?

And there we have it. Exactly the reason I didn't want to take this position in the first place. I am not your keeper, and I will not be responsible for everything you say and do.

When the tea ran out, Rhett brought us food. Meat, bread. He even offered us wine, but no-one wanted to risk that. Still, the food was well cooked and welcome. When Esther asked why a vampire would have supplies he didn't need to consume, his answer was simple: "Visitors." And he left it at that. There were no aromas around the house other than his own, so it was unlikely he'd had guests but given that I'm not Lou and didn't want to barrage him with twenty questions, I let it lie.

When we were full, he told us that the witch he knew about was under an hour's walk away, although we should probably wait until George felt his shoulder was healed enough to make the journey. Cue Lou and her questions. At least if I ever need to kill a few hours with a stranger again, I know exactly the person to take along with me.

"So, tell me," she started. "How long have you lived here …?"

A little before sunset, George decided he was up to the walk. To ensure his continued healing and keep the rest of us safe and alert to everything, we headed out as wolves, following Rhett. Wolf form also offered us the bonus of private conversation.

I don't get it, Lou's voice comes through clearly. *He said the walk was an hour, didn't he? But I can't smell any humans. We've been going for nearly that now, haven't we? We should be able to smell them by now, surely?*

She's right. If any human has ever walked this way, it must have been years ago. There's not even a trace of their scent.

Thus confirming my worries that this is a trap, Esther replies. *And we're about to be attacked by a vampire who's older than werewolves, impossibly strong and has had centuries to hone his combat skills, and yet we still don't have a plan.*

My plan is, we trust him, I finally snap.

We have no reason to trust him. It's only by luck that he didn't kill George.

He could have killed all of us. If I think we're in danger, I'll give the order to attack him, I swear on your lives, but we need allies. I'm not alienating him yet. And certainly not until we find out if he's telling the truth about this witch.

I don't want to get my expectations up, but as I imagine the possibility of finding help for Rey and bringing her back from whatever darkness Polidori sent her to, there's a flicker of hope in my heart. I know how hard she hunted for another witch herself, but maybe, in some grand scheme of existence, this is the universe's way of making sense of everything. If what happened between Oliver and me leads to us finding someone who can fix Rey, then it will have all been worth it in the end.

Unfortunately, the longer we walk without a hint of human in the air, the more and more I'm feeling Esther could be right about this whole escapade being a trap.

We're walking over more rocky terrain. There are pockets of sand which shifts beneath my paws and gets into my fur. As we near the top of a hill, Rhett pauses, possibly to say something, but I don't change back and give the order to the others to stay as they are. Then, as we reach the crest, a huddle of lights shines below us.

How? The question forms in our collective minds. *We couldn't smell it.*

The witch, I respond. *She must be able to cover her scent so vampires can't detect her.*

She's covered the scent of an entire village then, Esther adds.

A powerful witch, George comments in his normal, minimalistic style.

Maybe strong enough to get Rey back, I think, but I don't share this with the others. I can't get our hopes up yet.

We should change, I say, instead. *Walk the rest of the way in human form.*

Why? Witches and werewolves get on, don't they?

And vampires and wolves are supposed to be mortal enemies. I don't trust any of that. Rhett has carried clothes for us to change into. He must have thought it would be better for us to meet her as humans. Change.

I don't even need to say it's an order. It's somehow known, simply through the power of my thoughts, and a moment later, we're taking the clothes from Rhett.

"How are you feeling?" he asks me, as we descend the hill.

"Nervous," I admit. "Let's just say my recent interactions with a witch have been less than positive. And given that I've seen what even a new witch can do, I can't begin to imagine the power of this one."

"The masked scent, for example?"

He knows what I'm talking about immediately, although that's not a surprise. If my wolf's nose can't smell it, then there's a good chance his vampire one can't either.

"She masks her scent going to your house, too?"

"She does. Her magic can't do that for my scent quite as easily, though. The dead are apparently trickier to handle than the living, but people know where I am anyway. At least being able to cover up hers means that she can come and go freely."

So that explains the food back at his house and the comment about visitors. Not a quip, a genuine remark. A vampire who dines with a witch. Is it any weirder than one who sleeps with a werewolf, like Calin did? Probably not.

The journey down the hillside is quick, the paths well-trodden and easy to navigate, and it isn't long before we're standing in front of a small group of houses. Something about it reminds me of the North Pack village. The remoteness of it. The closeness of the homes. The feeling of warmth that emanates from within.

"You and your pack wait here," Rhett tells me, then walks towards one of the nearest houses.

Me and my pack. There may be only three of us, but it's still a pretty cool thing to hear said. Besides, I know it will be more. The minute the others are in range, Esther and George will tell them what's happened, and they will follow suit. Maybe I'll have to appoint a beta. Chrissie would be the obvious choice, as long as she's happy with it.

So, the four of us stand a little way back, remaining silent as Rhett knocks on the wooden door. There's a light on inside. A shadow ripples on the curtains as a figure crosses the window. The door opens.

"Rhett, I wasn't expecting you."

The voice is warm. She certainly doesn't sound upset by his presence, just a little confused.

"Is everything all right?"

"Vasara," he kisses her on both cheeks. "You look beautiful, as always. I apologise for the intrusion at this late hour, but I've brought some people to see you. People in need of help."

"What kind of help?"

"Your kind of help."

He steps aside, allowing us to set eyes on each other. Her face looks as kindly as her voice was, round and soft, her dark skin creased by age and laughter lines. Her hair hangs in tight ringlets that fall just below her shoulders. Like us, she is bare foot. Dozens of silver bangles stretch up her arms, jingling noisily as she brushes her hair from her face. As she looks past Rhett, her gaze falls on each of us in turn. It makes me feel exposed, in a way I have never experienced before.

"Wolves?" she says, with just the slightest hint of amusement playing on her features. "Well, you'd better come in and tell me all about it."

21

Calin

"This is ridiculous. They've been gone for four days. Why aren't the wolves out there looking for them? God knows what could have happened to them."

Oliver is pacing up and down the dining room, the same way he did yesterday and the day before that, the only difference today being how fast his strides are and how much swearing he's doing.

"This is fucking ridiculous. You know that, right? There are people after her, vampires who want her dead."

"I'm well aware of that. As is everybody in this house."

The sound of his teeth grinding together reverberates through his skull, and I can hear it from where I'm sitting all the way over on the other side of the room. Earlier today, he was out berating the wolves. Asking why they weren't doing anything. I know he's worried, but that was taking things a step too far. It's not as if they don't have enough to worry about. Hence, I ventured out into the daylight to drag him back inside. We've been going around and around the same point for the last half an hour, and it doesn't show any sign of abating.

"Try and take a bit of comfort from the fact that they're still here. I assume, if the worst-case scenario had happened, they would be able to sense it."

"Worst case scenario? You mean, as in they're dead? You know there are a hundred possibilities before it reaches that stage, all of which involve unthinkable pain and torture. Not to mention the fact that Naz isn't even part of the pack, so how would they be able to sense her? I just don't know why she had to run off like that. Why couldn't she at least have told someone where they were going?"

I watch the pain twist on his face, knowing that what he's saying is a lie. And knowing that he knows it, too. Vampire hearing can have its advantages, but that wasn't the case four days ago, when I would have preferred not to have it.

I should have seen it coming, though. I've not been oblivious to the way Oliver's heartbeat rises every time Narissa approaches. Nor how he would engineer things to ensure that she was never left alone with me. Not that she would have allowed anything to happen. No, I made my bed. Now I'm having to lie in it. Which, I guess, is why I feel just the tiniest bit of sympathy for him. He messed things up between them himself, but that doesn't mean he's not hurting.

"You're not to blame for her disappearing, you know," I say, as gently as I can.

Apparently not gently enough. He snaps his head around to face me, eyes narrowed, lips curled in a snarl.

"I bet you're just loving this, aren't you? I bet you're getting your kicks seeing how much I've screwed things up."

"No," I tell him truthfully. "My concern is for Narissa. For her happiness. That's all that matters to me."

He snorts, derisively, but there's less venom in the sound. He paces a few more times, then drops down onto the chair at the other end of the dining table.

"I just don't know how I'll forgive myself if something happens to her."

He speaks in a half whisper, his voice cracking in his throat. My sympathy extends a fraction further.

"You are not to blame for Narissa Knight's impulsive actions," I find myself saying. "She will be fine."

"But what if she's not?"

"She will be," I say, but it's not the first time I've said it. And now I'm starting to hear the uncertainty in my own voice. The row between the pair of them was heated, to put it mildly. At one point, I was worried she was going to turn wolf and rip him limb from limb. After how hurt she'd been at me lying to her and then finding out Oliver had done the same, it's no wonder she needed time to cool off. But there's time and there's time.

"I just wish I hadn't done it," Oliver says, his voice now heavy with sorrow.

"I understand. More than anyone, believe me."

We stay like this in silence. His heartbeat has slowed just a fraction, but I notice the way his hands clench and unclench as he grapples with a feeling of uselessness.

"Look, if she's not back by tomorrow, I'll go and talk to Chrissie myself," I say. "See if maybe she and I could go out together and try to pick up their scent."

He raises his head and offers a small nod. What then? I know he wants to ask. What happens if we don't find it? Or what if we do, and it leads us to discover she's been taken, or worse. But those are things I'll deal with if and when they arrive.

"Why don't you get yourself something to eat?" I say, standing up. "I promised Régine a turn in the garden."

I pause for a moment, thinking that perhaps he'll follow me out, but he remains seated, head in hands.

Régine's hospitality has been phenomenal, although I know from our conversations that she's found having the wolves here a blessing. Her home had once been so full of life, but that hadn't been the case for many years, until we arrived. The energy of the pack has imbued her with a new sense of purpose.

As her quarters are in the west wing of the chateaux, I normally cut through the kitchen, but for some reason, I find myself drawn to the front door.

The late afternoon sun sits low in the sky, just beyond the tree line. As I stare out into the distance, two wolves run out of the forest. I think at first that perhaps I've made a mistake. I'm not too great when it comes to distinguishing between them. In fact, there are only three I can comfortably recognise, and right now, I'm sure I'm looking at two of them.

"Oliver!" I shout. "Oliver!"

A moment later, he comes racing from the dining room. "What? What is it?"

"There," I point to the trees.

He stares, trying to work out what I'm talking about. I forget that his sight is not nearly as strong as mine. All the same, it doesn't take him long to realise.

"Is that …?"

"Naz and Lou. They're back. They're back."

While I might have the advantage of seeing further, he's able to run straight out into the open without needing to find a jacket, hat and gloves first, and he's already sprinting towards them.

He's not the only one who's excited. The wolves have already reached them and are now running around them in circles, heads up, howling. I've observed a fair bit of wolf behaviour over these past months, but nothing like this.

The moment I'm sufficiently covered, I race out, quickly catching up with him. As we arrive, the two wolves at the centre turn back to human.

"We've got ourselves an Alpha!" Lou shouts excitedly.

That explains their strange reaction. My instinct is to look at Narissa. There's a twinkle in her eye. Pride, I deduce. I can't help but think of Freya and how similar they look. Maybe, one day, she will allow me to tell her that.

"Wow, congratulations, Naz," Oliver says.

His voice is strained. Pained even. A pain that only increases when she doesn't even bother to acknowledge him. I'll give her that; she does a mean cold shoulder.

Ignoring both of us, she looks instead to the wolves, who are now all standing in human form, too.

"Yes, against my better judgement, I have accepted the position of Alpha," she says.

Cheers begin, but she raises a hand, and in an instant, they fall silent. It's impressive.

"There's no time for that, we've got something else to discuss. Something more important. While we were gone, we found a vampire."

I'm instantly on edge.

"An old vampire. His name is Rhett."

"Rhett?" Oliver repeats.

The name means nothing to him, but a murmur of disbelief sweeps through the wolves, a feeling I share. I've heard of Rhett, in connection with wolf mythology, but I assumed if he'd been real, he would have died centuries ago. If not, then he must be older than Polidori.

"There's more," Narissa continues, finally looking at me. "I'm afraid we will need to impose on Régine's kindness even more. I hope she won't mind."

"I doubt it," I say. "What's one more body."

"The thing is, it won't just be Rhett. He took us to meet someone. Someone who can help Rey."

CHAPTER 21

This time it's Oliver who's the one looking shocked, and she's looking straight at him.

"You found a witch?" he asks, the disbelief and hope in his voice impossible to disguise.

"No," she replies, as a car emerges from the forest, closely followed by a small minibus. "We didn't find a witch. We found a whole damned coven."

22

I will admit that whatever state I'd expected Narissa to return in, it was not like this. She's elated and laughing as she hugs Chrissie and the other wolves, offering introductions to the witches whose names she knows, apologising to those whose names she's not yet learned. Whether it's the effect of knowing what having them here could mean for Rey, or whether it's this new role of Alpha, she is glowing. She has more than enough to deal with, without me burning up in the sun, but as I retreat into the house, I'm well aware that I'm not alone.

"Calin, I assume?" he says, when we're safely within the shadow of the house. Not that it appears to make any difference to him. His bare arms are enough to make me overheat just looking at them. "Naz told me about you. I'm Rhett." He holds out a hand, which I shake. "You're a member of the Council, isn't that right?"

"I suspect my membership may have been revoked," I reply, flatly.

He smiles.

"Perhaps we could go and talk somewhere?"

"That might be wise."

We make our way to the snug behind the kitchen, and I pick up a bottle of Pinot Noir and two glasses on the way. Providing a visitor with refreshment is as customary for vampires as it is for humans. Red wine felt like the most reasonable substitute to what would normally be offered, if only in appearance.

"This is an unusual set-up you have here," Rhett observes.

"Says the vampire who's been consorting with witches," I counter.

"I never said my situation was any the less unusual."

He takes a small sip of his drink. Perhaps he's concerned I might have put something in it. We're sitting in opposite armchairs, but there isn't much room between us; this room is called a snug for a reason.

"So, you and the witches, you are … friends?" I ask.

"In some cases, yes. In others, I would like to think I'm more than that. I've been in some of their lives since they were born. Since before their grandparents were born, in fact."

"Is that so?"

"It is."

I understand what he's telling me. He's a good guy. He sides with witches, and that means he can't be a fan of other vampires. He wants me to know that.

"And now you're here. So what happened? Narissa just

asked, and you got the witches to pack up their coven and follow her? Just like that? What do you get from it?"

I realise I'm being very blunt, but we've both been around too long to pussy-foot.

"It's not about me. It's about the witches. After her parents passed, Vasara made it her mission to provide a sanctuary for as many of them as she could. It's not an exaggeration to say that she's travelled around the world more than once to help a fellow witch. This journey was comparatively short."

"And you always come along for the ride?"

There's a slight glimmer in his eyes, as if he's enduring my questioning in the same way a parent would that of a toddler which, compared to him, I suppose I am.

I'm still awaiting an answer when the door swings open.

Beside Narissa is an older woman, who I detect is a witch. Unlike the usual stereotype, she wears her hair in shoulder length curls that seem almost luminous, and as cheesy as it may sound, there's something quite enchanting about her. Rhett's eyes linger on her, as if he too is seeing her for the first time, although that's obviously not the case.

"So, this is where you're hiding," Narissa says.

A moment passes and I realise I should probably speak.

"Vasara, I assume?" I say, standing and stretching out my hand.

She takes it and shakes it tentatively. Not weakly, just as if she's used to greetings other than handshakes.

"And you must be Calin. Narissa has mentioned you."

Narissa looks at Rhett.

"How much have you said to him? Have you told him about Polidori's visit?"

"We weren't yet past the formalities," Rhett grins at her, before also standing up and offering his seat to Vasara, who takes it. As Narissa steps in, I wonder if I should do the same and offer her my seat, but given how we've been the last couple of months, I think she's more likely to hit me than thank me. I'm shifting a little further away, making it clear I'm not going to use it again, when another figure appears.

"Is this a private meeting?" Oliver asks, his eyes scanning the group.

"Yes," Narissa says. "So come in and close the door. You should hear all this, too."

The surprised expression on his face indicates he hadn't expected that to be her answer. He hurries in, closing the door behind him, as if he's worried she might change her mind.

When the door is closed, I turn to Rhett.

"You met with Polidori?" I ask. "When? Why? What did he want?"

Rhett looks at Vasara before he responds. It's a long, lingering look in which a dozen different things could have been communicated. I've not heard of witches using telepathy, but if these two have been friends long enough, perhaps they don't need it.

"I'm afraid I can't tell you what he wanted," Rhett says, eventually.

Anger flashes through me. Red hot and fierce. He reads it instantly.

"You misunderstand me. I'm not saying I wouldn't tell you. I just don't know. He turned up on my doorstep, apparently to tell me about some interesting *developments*. I think that was the word he used. He said it didn't just involve vampires; there were wolves involved, too. He wanted me to hear him out."

"Well, why didn't you?"

It's Oliver who asks the question, but it's exactly the same one I was thinking.

"Because of me," Vasara answers, and all eyes turn to her. "I was visiting Rhett. By the time he heard him coming, there was no way I could safely leave. I can mask my scent, but there would still have been the risk of him seeing me. He wouldn't have needed to know I was witch, to decide I was worthy of becoming his supper."

"The Head of the Council?" I say.

I know there's now so much evidence pointing to the contrary, but the Polidori who raised me cared for humans. I'm having trouble adjusting to the fact that it may have all been a facade.

"You need to remember, I knew him before all that," Rhett replies. "I knew him when he raided villages. When he would drain a witch to the point of near death, only to let her recover and experience the same torture over and over again. I couldn't have him finding Vasara there. If I'd tried to pass her off as a blood donor, my home would have shown me to be a liar. You saw what it was like," he says to Narissa.

"It was human friendly," she answers.

"Exactly. I needed him gone. So, I told him in no

uncertain terms to leave. The next day, I set traps to protect myself. Vasara has rarely left the village since then."

Oliver and Narissa's disappointment is palpable, as is mine. To have known what Polidori was up to would have made it a darn sight easier to stop him.

"The good news," Narissa says, with the smile returning to her face, "is that maybe he told Rey what he was planning. And now we have Vasara, we can get her back."

I notice the glance she exchanges with Oliver. It's involuntary, like anything she says about Rey must be run by him first. Looking at him still seems to cause her pain, just as it does with me.

"That sounds like a plan," Vasara says, "although would it be possible to get something to eat first? I'm afraid we're all rather hungry. We avoided stopping on the way here."

As if on cue, the bell that signals dinner is ready rings through the house. Once more, Narissa's smile returns.

"Don't worry. You won't be hungry for long."

23

Narissa

At dinner, Régine was surprisingly relaxed with the fact that yet another dozen people were imposing on her hospitality.

"I don't think I can let Henri do all the cooking every day, though," she said after a moment surveying the scene in front of her. "Poor man nearly has a heart attack trying to get all the food ready at once, and that was when it was just the wolves. We'll have to come up with alternative dinner arrangements."

"Really, Régine, you don't have to worry about feeding us wolves, we've told you that already," Chrissie says. "And we can sleep outside. It's not a problem."

"Outside? In this weather? Don't be ridiculous. I've got half a dozen empty cottages around the estate. Of course, they're not all in the most habitable condition, but I'm sure a quick sweep through and a few throw rugs will help. I've often thought that I should do something with them. You know, convert them. Turn them into holiday homes perhaps. That's what all the trendy folk do these days, isn't it? But what do I need with all that hassle? Just thinking about all that work makes me want to lie down. It's not like I need the money."

"Whatever space you've got, we'll be grateful for. We can camp together."

"Well, I'll get Henri to show you and our new guests the different options. Although not until you've eaten, obviously. He'll be furious if I let any of this go to waste."

ONCE AGAIN, HENRI'S PREPARED A BLOODY BANQUET. How the hell he put all this together is a miracle, although his swearing had been audible from all corners of the chateaux before the dinner bell rang, and I'm pretty certain the chicken coop will be missing a few birds.

Rhett has been welcomed with a mixture of suspicion and complete adoration. Suspicion mainly from the male wolves in the pack, possibly due to the adoration of the females. Even Chrissie is in awe.

"So how did you come to be friends with a vampire?" Oliver asks Vasara over after-dinner coffee.

We're sitting at the other end of the table to Rhett and the wolves. Calin and Régine have taken the other witches on a tour of the place, and I'm grateful that Vasara declined the invitation. I've had no opportunity to speak to her alone since we met, and there's a lot I want to find out. But I'm not the only one, and telling Oliver to leave, just because I don't want him near me, doesn't seem right. Having her here does help to diffuse the tension between us.

"Rhett has been a friend to my coven longer than I've been alive. I've known him my whole life. He's family … no, much more than that. He will be able to tell you in his own words, but he took a vow to himself to preserve life, whether it be human, wolf or witch."

"Not vampire?"

"He tends not to talk about it much, but for whatever reason, I think it's fair to say he's not a fan of his own kind."

"How did he find your coven? And how had you survived? I thought the vampires outlawed them and they'd all been eliminated."

"Most witches were murdered, you're correct. It's down to Rhett that we survived. He hid my great grandmother and her two sisters when they tried to purge our kind. He kept them hidden for years, until the hunting had died down. Then, as they were able to get back to a more normal existence and numbers grew, he continued to keep vampires away. Those of his kind who know he's still alive, give the area a wide berth. Those who don't know him and come our way don't really stand a chance. And the last place any would think to look for witches is near one of the oldest vampires still in existence."

It makes perfect sense. Essentially, Rhett has been operating as their guard dog. And it's obviously worked.

"So, you do magic." Oliver says, seeming to feel the need to state the obvious. "Proper witchcraft."

"We do. Mostly earth magic. Manipulation of the elements—like the way we erase our scent, so we can't be tracked."

It's an amazing skill to have and one I'd certainly like to borrow. To be able to mask my scent from Polidori and the other vampires who want me dead, would definitely make me feel a whole heap safer. Still, that's only one spell. I'm keen to know what else they can do. And more importantly, how she can help Rey.

"Where do your spells come from?" I ask her. "Do you still have grimoires?"

She shakes her head and sighs.

"What we have, has been passed down more recently and informally, mostly learned through trial and error, and there has always been much error involved. Some attempts to increase our knowledge have had their … how do I put this? Idiosyncrasies. Obviously, we write everything down so that we have some small, what you might call, grimoires of our own. They are just notebooks really. The larger books, the real ancient tomes … well, I assume you know about those."

"The vampires took them."

"They did. My grandmother was young when Rhett saved her. She and her sisters were lucky to escape with their lives, let alone any belongings. But we've been lucky. We've had time. Time when it has been safe to practise and learn. We keep adding to our knowledge, and each generation of us is stronger than the last."

"Strong enough to erase the dark magic that's taken hold of our friend?" I ask.

She looks at me with sympathy—an almost maternal tenderness—and for a second, images of Freya spring to mind. I blink them away before they can take hold.

"I think it's probably time I met this friend of yours. Don't you?"

24

"I want to be in there, too. I should be with her."

"You'd be a distraction. Trust Vasara. She knows what she's doing. She said she's got this. Besides, the three of us can keep watch from here. If anything goes wrong, we'll be right there."

If anything goes wrong. I feel sick. My stomach is churning with worry, but at the same time, I'm excited and full of optimism.

"It's likely the dark magic may try to resist me at first," Vasara told me before she headed to the old coal store. "That's okay. I'll work with it. I'll get through to her. She was only practising for a few months, correct?"

"Yes, she was with another witch that the vampires had working for them. Four months maybe. And then her time here with us."

"That's fine. It will not have had the chance to become deep rooted."

She'd clasped my hands, squeezing tightly before releasing them.

"You will have your friend back soon."

Then she was gone, and I came to this small room where the CCTV monitor is set up. Calin and Oliver were already waiting. The three of us are together in a very small space. What should be a horribly awkward situation has been diluted as each of us has their eyes locked on the screen. Oliver and I are almost holding our breath in anticipation, as the door to the shed opens and Vasara steps inside.

Rey is sitting on the bed, her arms and legs still shackled, although she can move around a little. She lifts her head and frowns quizzically as Vasara approaches.

"I don't know you," she says.

Her words are factual, slightly dismissive but spoken with no more disdain than she addresses anyone these days.

"You arrived yesterday. I guess that means there are even more wolves here now."

Vasara offers a small chuckle. Warm. Not condensing. Endearing. She has this wonderful softness about her, and I find myself momentarily wondering what she must have been like when she was young.

"No, not wolves. Your friends found me. Found us. They brought me here to help you."

"Friends?"

A cackle rises from Rey's throat as she displays her manacled hands.

"This is not a place where I have friends. What are you,

CHAPTER 24

some kind of supernatural shrink, planning on talking my power away? Believe me, they've tried."

It's hard to see their facial expressions with the limited view of the camera. Vasara takes a moment before she speaks again. Her hands rest causally at her side, and she tilts her head, as if surveying Rey from a different angle.

"You can't tell?" she says, eventually.

"Tell what?"

Without answering her question, Vasara crosses to the other side of the room and returns with a chair in her hands. It's the one Oliver frequently sits on to talk to her. I've seen Calin in there too sometimes when I've been unable to sleep and have found myself wandering the house in the early hours. From what I've seen, he never speaks to her, just sits there, ready to listen should she decide to talk.

After placing the chair closer to Rey than I would ever dare, Vasara sits down, reaches a hand into a pocket and pulls out a small paper packet.

"What's that?" Oliver says, stiffening beside me. "What's she going to do to her?"

"I don't know any more than you. Just wait."

"I should be down there with her."

"Just wait, will you?" I say, grabbing his wrist. "Trust her. She's good."

His posture remains tense. He's ready to move but waits, his eyes glued to the monitor, waiting for what is about to happen. I'm still holding him, my fingertips on his skin. He, too, seems to notice this first touch we've shared.

His attention moves to my hand and then to my face. Feeling a tightening in my stomach, I let go of him and refocus on the screen.

Vasara, still seated, tips the contents of the bag into her hand.

"Are those seeds?" Oliver asks.

"I believe so," Calin responds.

We're not the only ones who are intrigued. Rey is observing the stranger with a new sense of curiosity.

"I'd like to show you something," Vasara says. "You see, I'm like you."

She returns all the seeds to the packet except one, which she leaves on her open palm. She stretches out her hand for Rey to see it.

"*Augti kartu su gamta. Augu su sviesa. Augti kartu su gamta. Augu su sviesa.*"

The grain vibrates on her hand. Then a green tendril sprouts from it.

"*Augti kartu su gamta. Augu su sviesa.*"

Vasara continues her chant, her eyes on the seed, that's becoming a seedling, growing larger as we watch. She tightens her fist around the roots that have formed and the first leaf bursts open, quickly followed by another. It's standing nearly a foot tall in her hand when a bud forms. Slowly, the sepals open and bright white petals bloom.

"You're a witch," Rey says.

Her words are unsteady, and she seems to be trembling. For the first time since she found us, I can see something resonating deeply within her, hopefully deeper than whatever it was the vampires did to her. This was all she ever wanted. Witches. Family. Her own kind. She blinks, still staring at the plant in Vasara's hand, which has now grown more blooms.

There are tears in my eyes. Tears of hope. Of love. A hand reaches out and squeezes mine. Calin's. And because the moment is what it is, I don't let go.

"Yes, I am a witch," Vasara says, answering her question. "There are several of us here. We heard you needed help."

If Rey can hear what's being said to her, she chooses not to respond. Instead, she stretches out her fingers. There's only so far she can reach, bound as she is, but Vasara can tell, just as well as we can, what she wants and moves the flowers towards her. Tentatively, Rey touches the edge of one of the petals.

The effect is instantaneous. In a heartbeat, it turns black, curling in on itself. One after another, all the petals curl and turn crisp, blackening as if held to a flame. The leaves and stem go next, withering before our very eyes until all that remains in Vasara's palm is a sooty skeleton. The witch shifts quickly back, fear in her eyes.

"I guess that was not what you intended," Rey says, with a smirk. "But the spell was an interesting one. What did you say it was? *Augti kartu su gamta. Augu su sviesa.?* Yes, that was it, wasn't it? *Augti kartu su gamta. Augu su sviesa. Augti kartu su gamta. Augu su sviesa.*"

Her hands become claw like as she extends her palms out towards the walls. The look of shock and fear on Vasara's face suddenly deepens.

"Can you feel that?" Calin asks, releasing my hand. "I can hear something."

We don't have time to register what it is he's noticed. Vasara is on her feet, arms held up to the ceiling as she chants.

"*Istremkite tamsa, ileista i sviesa. Istremkite tamsa, ileista i sviesa.*"

Her voice rises, louder and louder, but it's not enough to drown out Rey, or the rumbling that seems to be coming from the earth itself. We continue watching, not knowing what to do. The image on the screen begins to disappear. The whole room is being covered in leaves, thick dense ivy.

"*Augti kartu su gamta. Augu su sviesa.*"

"Rey's producing this," Oliver says, fear in his voice. "What do we do? Do we leave Vasara with her?"

"It's the dark magic resisting her. She said this might happen. She said to wait."

"*Istremkite tamsa, ileista i sviesa.*"

The older witch's chanting continues, as she tries to outperform Rey. Vasara must be the stronger of the two. She's had years of practice. She's grown up mastering the art. And yet the leaves have now obscured the camera to the point where we can barely see them anymore.

"What do we do?" Oliver says again. "Surely we can't leave her like this. We need to go in and help her."

"She said to wait."

The screen is now completely dark, and the chanting is growing fainter as leaves smother the microphone, too. My knuckles are white, my nails digging into the palms of my hands as I wait. Wait for the leaves to retreat. For Vasara to beat the dark magic. Then Calin's voice shudders through the air.

"Something's wrong," he says. "I'm going in."

"No, you must wait!"

I move to stop him, but he's already gone.

25

Vasara

When I grew up, magic was as normal to me as food and laughter. My parents never hid their powers and when I was older, they used to boast that I'd been able to perform magic before I said my first words. Now, I realise the impossibility of that. In all my life, I've never known a witch, child or otherwise, who was able to utter a successful incantation in anything other than clear words. At the time, I was happy to bask in their praise. But true or not, I was aware from an early age that I was strong. Stronger than any other witch I knew.

When I first started, it was with small spells, like making water boil or hastening the flow of a stream. Later, came more complicated ones, like changing the leaves on a tree from green to rust red or making it rain on a sweltering summer's day. I recall those moments as clear as day, the same way I remember the first time I encountered black magic. The *only* time that ever happened, before this place.

Whether it was normal or simply a twist of fate, all the women born in our village possessed stronger magical powers than the men. Two generations in, and it was regarded as a matter of fact, and no one seem to mind. And then August was born.

Even as a young boy, it was clear that his strength matched that of his female peers. But August didn't want to match anyone. August wanted to be superior.

He was younger than me, by ten years or so, and at first I saw nothing but eagerness to learn in the way he would follow me around, asking me questions, seeking my help and badgering me to watch him perform simple spells. This continued all the way up to his teenage years, at which point he withdrew, normal behaviour for a boy of that age, I thought. This was what they all did, withdrew for a few years, seeking independence until they were ready to join forces again.

Even when I saw his sullen ways at coven feasts and festivals—so unlike the vibrancy with which we live our daily lives, let alone at such events—I thought little of it, other than how pleased I'd be when he grew out of this phase and returned to us fully, with his heart as well as his presence. That was until the day he came rushing towards the village, carrying my nephew in his arms.

"Help! Help me!"

We heard his cries before he'd even crested the hill. I was outside at the time, trying to devise a simple levitation spell from a mixture of incantations I already knew. It's still not something I've mastered, despite countless attempts through the years. I suspect that, unless by a miracle I manage to get my hands on some of the great, old grimoires, it will continue to best me. Still, I digress. I didn't notice it was August who was screaming at first, I was so focused on the body in his arms. My sister's young son.

"Phillip!"

I scrambled up the hill towards them, not waiting to see if any of the elders were following.

"Phillip, what's the matter? What happened to him?"

His body was limp and his skin ashen. Shallow breaths wheezed from his lips.

"I didn't mean to do it," August cried. "I can't switch it off. I can't stop it."

That was when I looked at him. His hands were trembling and tears were trickling down his cheeks, but his eyes … after all these years, I still haven't found a word to describe what I saw there or, more accurately, what I didn't see. It was as if there was no soul beyond his pupils. Just a nothingness, a bleak void.

As I stood there, mesmerised, the elders appeared behind me and started chanting the words, *Augti kartu su gamta. Augu su sviesa.* Banish the darkness, let in the light. *Augti kartu su gamta. Augu su sviesa.* As their voices came to a crescendo, the very ground on which we stood trembled. I could feel the power seeping from August and returning to the earth, where it belonged. I could see it fading from the empty eyes. And as the darkness left him, so life returned to Phillip.

Later, we learned he'd been practising for years, switching out words in incantations we knew well, such light for dark, love for hate, life for death, hoping he would stumble upon new, more powerful spells. And he succeeded with his plan, but on that day we nearly lost Phillip, he realised the truth about black magic. While what we practice is at one with the world, the dark arts work against it. While we give, they only take and take and take. They will strip you of whatever humanity you have and then demand more.

I cannot say what he felt that day, how it affected him to be so close to a precipice, but what I do know is that he never practised magic again, of any kind. He took to tending the farm, the animals in particular, and never, until the day he passed, did I hear him utter another single incantation.

That was my only experience of black magic. Until today.

26

Narissa

I race after Calin as fast as my human legs will carry me. I'm strong now, the strongest I've been in my whole life, but it's not enough. I need to get there faster. I need to be with Rey.

When I finally reach the door, I freeze and my breath catches in my lungs. Rey is draped across Calin's arms, her body limp, her eyes rolled back.

"She's fine," he says, but there's a sense of urgency in his voice. "Help Vasara. Get those vines off her."

I look past him and see she's bound in foliage. The whole room is overrun with ivy. The vines have emerged through cracks which are zigzagging across the walls. It's a miracle the little coal store hasn't collapsed. Gasping on the floor, Vasara is grappling with the plants

CHAPTER 26

that have twisted themselves around her throat and chest.

"Here, I've got this. Let me help you."

I drop to the ground and grab at the stalks. Not since I was cage fighting have I managed to summon up the strength of the wolf while still in human form, but I'm now tearing at the vines in an adrenalin-powered frenzy. One comes away and then another, but there are so many of them. As I reach and break off the last one from around her throat, I hear a sharp intake of breath.

"It's okay," I say, pulling away more foliage from her chest and legs.

Finally free, Vasara rolls onto her hands and knees. She stays like this, panting for a few moments before pushing back onto her heels. Her eyes are bloodshot. Her skin is pale and blotchy, and when she speaks, her voice is raw.

"Thank you," she says to me before turning to Calin. "Venom, I assume."

He nods, concern clouding his face.

"I'm amazed she's not immune to it by now, the amount she's had."

"I, for one, am thankful she's not," Vasara says, pushing herself up onto her feet. I cup a hand under her elbow to offer a little help.

"Really, it's fine. Nothing is hurt, other than my pride."

She attempts a smile, but it falls flat, barely even a flicker on her lips.

"What happened?" I whisper. "I thought you could help her."

"So did I. But black magic feeds off negative energy—

hatred, hurt, pain—and it has taken a very strong hold on her. For it to happen like this, I cannot imagine what spells she's done in her time. You must have been wrong about how long she was practising, and she must have been a powerful witch for the vampires to be interested in her."

I shake my head.

"She didn't even know she was a witch until quite recently. She read one spell out loud from a grimoire, and it ruined her whole life."

Vasara's eyes widen.

"Then this power …"

She doesn't even manage to finish her sentence.

"You probably don't need me to tell you that I didn't get through to her. The healing incantations that I know, are not enough."

The pain of failure flashes through me, but I still have hope.

"That was just you," I say, optimistically. "We could use the other witches too, couldn't we? Doesn't your power get stronger when there a more of you acting together?"

I realise I'm basing this on late-night fantasy television shows, but it feels logical.

"Your friend fed off my strength. I could feel it happening. If the other witches joined me, who knows what power she'd be able to garner. Besides, there's another issue. Like I said to you before, without the grimoires to guide us, many of our spells have imperfections. When we perform an incantation together, we're bound together. What affects one of us, affects all of us. I can't take the risk."

Disappointment curdles within me. Finding them, a

whole coven of witches just when we needed them the most, felt as if fate might actually be on our side for once. Turns out it's just got a seriously sadistic sense of humour.

"So that's it then. There's nothing you can do?"

"Not at the moment. There are counter spells to all black magic, of that I'm certain, but I don't have access to such knowledge."

It's like a knife twisting in my gut. If Vasara can't save her, then no one can. I look at Rey, now lying motionless on the bed, her breathing so shallow she looks almost lifeless. And yet, like this, with her eyes closed, she looks so like my old friend. How can I give up on her? I don't think I can.

"What about the original grimoires?" Calin asks.

He, too, is staring at Rey.

"If you had spells from the older grimoires, the ones the vampires took, might you be able to help her then?"

Vasara takes a deep breath and I assume yet more bad news is to follow, but she nods ever so slightly.

"It's possible. Likely, I'd say. If the spells we need are going to be anywhere, then they'll be in those books."

Her words hang in the air among us, and I wonder who's thinking the same as me, who else is contemplating the unthinkable.

"Well then, that's settled," Calin says. "We need to go and get those grimoires."

And for once, I don't disagree.

27

"Will you all stop shouting!"

At my raised voice, the wolves all fall silent, but unfortunately the alpha trick doesn't work on the witches or Calin and Oliver, both of whom have been vocal with their opinions since this meeting started. In fact, considering I'm the one who called it, I've barely managed to get a word in edgeways. But time is slipping away, and the sooner we can get on with this, the better. So, if pulling my leader card helps us get it done, then that's what I'll do.

It's been a busy morning, mostly filled with conversations with Rhett, Vasara and Calin and all under the weight of tiredness and failure. Last night, I fell asleep in my chair watching Rey on the small screen, This wasn't my plan at all although avoiding my bedroom, where Oliver and I slept together the last night I was here, might have been at the back of my mind.

The dose of venom Calin gave her was one of the biggest so far. She didn't utter a word all night. Even after I woke up this morning, showered and returned, she was still lying in the same position. She is breathing, though. I'll go back and check on her again after I'm done here. She probably needs to eat something, too. If Vasara is anything to go by, using strong magic is pretty depleting.

I glower at everyone, and finally the rest of the voices die down.

"This is not up for discussion," I say firmly. "We're going ahead, with or without everyone's approval. This explanation of what's going to happen is merely a curtesy."

While this statement is directed at everyone, it particularly applies to Oliver, who's sulking. When we took the idea to him earlier, he spent a long time trying to convince us that the copies of the grimoires held at Blackwatch would be sufficient. Even after Vasara had explained that the pages of the originals would be imbued with power from the witches who wrote them, he still wasn't convinced.

"I'm going to take a small team and break into the vaults of the Vampire Council and steal the grimoires we need," I continue. "We still don't know what Polidori is planning, but with the new vampires he's been siring and Juliette's pack under his thumb, it can't be good. Rey may be the only option we have to find out before it's too late."

"Surely, breaking into their building is a suicide mission? Won't they sense you straight away?" comes from one of the pack.

"The vampires won't be a problem. There won't be any guards and Polidori will be far too occupied to worry about us."

"How can you be so sure?"

This time it's a witch who speaks up. These are not dissenting voices, but they do understand how much is at risk.

"Because he'll be dealing with me," Rhett says.

"Polidori has wanted Rhett on his side for years," I explain, addressing them all. "Rhett's already sent him word that he wants a meeting and that he will see him at their headquarters but only if no one else at all is there."

"Being a recluse has its advantages," Rhett says, with a small smile. "When you make strange requests like having a building empty, people just assume it's one of your quirks."

"Have you heard from Polidori? Have you got word back from him yet?"

"No." Rhett shakes his head. "And I don't expect to. I told him when I would be arriving and that should be enough. If he doesn't adhere to my request, we simply abort."

"So, Rhett keeps Polidori occupied. Then what?" Chrissie asks.

"Calin, Vasara and I will go down into the vaults and find the grimoires."

"No." Oliver shakes his head immediately. "It's too risky. You have your pack to think about, Naz. I'll go instead."

This comes out as an order, and if it was just the pair of us talking, I'd shoot him down in an instant, but I get the feeling his pride is on a knife's edge at the moment. Besides, I'd be lying if I said I didn't know he'd be angry. Not just about what the plan entails, but the fact I didn't consult him on it until most of the details had already been agreed.

"Taking a human is too much of a risk," I say. "Calin knows the way, so he must go. He'll guide Vasara and me to the vaults. I'll be there so I can turn wolf if anything goes wrong. Which it shouldn't because, like I said, Rhett's going to have Polidori covered for us."

The plan sounds straight forward in my mind, but I can tell from the looks around me I'm in for some blowback.

"Oliver is right, you're the Alpha now." Esther, as always, is the first to pipe up. "You're the only one of us wolves who is not expendable."

There's a roar of agreement which I quickly wave down.

"No one here is any more expendable than I am. You know that. And I am only Alpha by default."

"You're still the Alpha."

"And aren't alphas the ones that take the risks?"

"Yes, for their pack. But this isn't for the pack."

This last comment comes from somewhere near the back of the room and though I can't see directly who said it, it doesn't matter. Judging by the way silence falls, the sentiment is obviously shared. Rey's not part of the pack and therefore not worth risking their alpha's life for.

"Regardless of what you think and what the rules might have been before now, Rey is a member of the only family I had for a long time and before I even knew I was a wolf. By extension, she's also a member of our pack."

A murmur rumbles through them. It's my word on the matter, whether they like it or not. I pause, considering how much I should share next.

"Most of you know this …" I say, trying to fend off

tears. "I led Rey into the situation where she was taken by the vampires who then turned her into whatever it is she's become. I know what you're all thinking. I know that you want to work together for vengeance for Freya and the pack. I understand that is your ultimate goal. I respect that and promise we *will* get there. But this first step, getting these grimoires and freeing Rey, is what I have to do. Now, if anyone disagrees so much that they want to challenge me for Alpha, then I'll gladly hand over."

I wait. Nothing. Just dozens of eyes looking at the ground.

"Okay then. This must happen with me. My word on this is final."

I turn to leave, when Lou's voice stops me.

"At least take one of us with you. If the vampires are alerted, one more wolf on your side has got to be a good thing."

Voices of agreement quickly rise.

"We could go in as a pack. They'd have no defence then."

"Or take half of us. The other half could stay here to protect Rey and the other witches."

Lou looks at me, her eyes pleading. She's already lost a brother, although not in death, but it still can't be easy. I know losing me too would be harder for her than I can imagine. Fortunately, I have no intention of dying there.

"We'll discuss it," I say, looking to Vasara, Calin and Rhett so they know who I'm referring to.

I march out the room, well aware of the fact that someone is hot on my heels. There's no way I can escape this conversation, as much as I want to. Not that I owe him anything.

"Naz," he calls from behind, but I keep up my pace and head outside.

The last thing I want is a whole coven and a wolf pack listening in.

"Naz, please, talk to me."

I keep going until I'm far enough away from the house that only the two vampires would be able to hear what's being said although, hopefully, they'd have enough decency not to tune in.

"You can't think this is a good idea," Oliver says when I finally stop. "Please, at least let me go with you."

I slowly turn around to face him. For someone who I always thought of as so impervious to worry, I don't know how I never noticed all his insecurities before. Then again, maybe I'm the one who helped put them there.

"I need you here. If anything were to happen, I need you to keep fighting for Rey."

"And that's all it is?"

"Of course. This is about Rey, Oliver and that's all I've got the energy to focus on right now."

I feel my poker face is pretty impressive, yet Oliver continues to scrutinise me before he shakes his head with a sigh. When he speaks, it's clear he doesn't buy it. Even if it is a half-truth.

"You don't want to be near me. I get it. But you can't put yourself in danger, just because of that—"

"Oliver, I would be in more danger worrying about you there. This isn't personal. This … this stuff between us …

we'll talk about it when I get back. You don't have to worry, I'll be protected by Calin and the oldest, most experienced vampire who's ever existed, not to mention a strong witch."

"A witch who couldn't even protect herself from Rey."

My hands land on my hips.

"What do you want me to say, Oliver? That I won't go? That I'll send one of my wolves in my place? You should know me well enough to realise I'm not going to change my mind on this."

A look of defeat settles on his face.

"Please, think about what Lou said, then. If you won't let me go with you, at least take another wolf."

I nod and mean it when I say, "I'll think about it."

28

We travel by car to the ferry point. It's a long way from the luxury of the private helicopter Calin hired for Oliver to get me out of danger in Scotland. It's also a lot less conspicuous.

I took Lou's advice, although much to her dismay, it was Esther I asked to accompany us. Lou's just too big a risk, not to mention she'd make me vulnerable. I've learned the hard way that having people you feel responsible for on missions like this only makes it harder. Of course, Calin is with me too, but I try not to think about that.

So that means there are five of us cramped into the small car heading to Calais.

Vasara is driving and Rhett is sitting next to her. To pass the time, I try to work out exactly what the relationship is between the pair of them. She appears older, clearly in her fifties, but obviously that means nothing in real terms. Every now and then, I see his eyes drift across to her, and there's definitely a sense of something going on there.

A longing maybe, love even. Certainly more than friendship, although there's no awkwardness there, unlike me and Calin.

Esther is sitting in the middle of the back seat between us, like an uncomfortable chaperone on a couple's first date. This living barrier doesn't disguise the fact that Calin and I haven't said two words to each other since we started out. However, the closer we get to the port, the less I worry about him and focus on what we're about to undertake.

The last few miles, we've been travelling through towns, on roads busy with cars and lorries. Other people make me nervous. It's daytime, but that wouldn't stop Juliette's wolves. Vasara may have masked her scent, but she said the spell doesn't work quiet so well on vampires, so a keen nose might well be able to detect them.

As we enter the port gates and the ferry comes into view, my nerves ramp up another notch.

"Are you sure this is going to work?" I check. "Polidori has probably got people in every port looking out for us."

"Trust me, this is a spell I know I can do."

Vasara closes her eyes and mutters under her breath. I shouldn't disturb her, but I'm in need of a little reassurance. The moment she stops chanting, I ask again.

"Just go over it one more time with me."

A small sigh escapes Esther's lips, but I ignore it. Call it alpha prerogative, but if I need to hear this another hundred times, then I will.

"It's similar to the incantation we use to hide a scent. And it's totally reliable. It was one of the first spells written down by our family."

"And it will make us invisible?"

"No, it will just make us one hundred percent forgettable. You can still be seen, but you'll have one of those faces that just disappears from the mind the moment you're out of sight. A person could look at you, see every one of your features, and yet the second you're gone, they wouldn't be able to say if your eyes were blue or green or whether your hair was shaved or long and curly, if they remember you at all. You'll just slip from their consciousness."

One hundred percent forgettable. That feels uncannily familiar. It's exactly how I felt before all this shit started happening.

"You don't need to worry," Calin says. "I can't smell any vampires here. Rhett and I will be monitoring this."

"Okay. Time for passports everybody," Rhett says, twisting over his shoulder and grinning.

And another slice of magic is dished up. Just a piece of paper and an enchantment ensures the person looking at it sees whatever they're expecting or wanting. Vasara used it on me before we got in the car, making me believe that an old shopping receipt was a fifty Euro note. No wonder these witches didn't need jobs. Why bother when you can pull stunts like that?

All the same, butterflies are swarming inside me as the border control officer takes the blank pieces of paper. A minute later, our car is rumbling up the metal ramp onto the ferry.

We follow directions to our parking space and Vasara cuts the engine

"Okay, it all smells good so far," Rhett says, before

unbuckling his seat belt. "But I'm going to walk around and make sure there's nothing I've missed. Anyone else want to join me?"

Vasara nods and unclips her belt.

"Sounds good. I could do with a drink, too."

He smiles, like he knew she'd say that.

"I'll cast a shrouding spell, so no one knows you're down here."

Following the short incantation, the two of them leave the three of us in the backseat of the car. Never has the expression *three's a crowd* felt more apt. The question is how to remove the third wheel.

"Esther, do you not what to join them?" I say as casually as I can manage.

"I think I'll stay here," she replies and leans her head back. "I tend to get a bit seasick on boats."

"Then maybe some fresh air would do you good. It's kinda stuffy down here."

"It's okay."

I grit my teeth and force myself to smile.

"Seriously, think about it."

She opens her mouth to respond when the penny finally drops. Her jaw snaps closed, and for a moment, I sense her embarrassment.

"You know what," she says, unbuckling herself, "I think I might just go for a walk after all. Yeah, let me just squeeze past you."

I step out of the car, pushing myself against the door to give her enough room to leave, before sliding back into my seat.

CHAPTER 28

And then it's just me and Calin. This is what I wanted, and yet now that it's happened, I feel my heart race. For months, I've been a complete and utter bitch, and I know there's only one thing I should say, but that doesn't mean it's easy. My nails are digging into the palms of my hands as I suck in a deep breath.

"I owe you a massive apology."

The words blurt out in a stream, before I can chicken out. But the way his eyes widen in surprise, makes me feel I've said something wrong.

"I'll admit that wasn't how I was expecting this conversation to go," he says. "I'm pretty sure I'm the one who should have started with that."

"No. You've already tried. I know you have. I just wouldn't hear it."

He nods slowly. The temperature in the car, down here in the bowels of the ferry, is warm, yet for some reason I'm incredibly cool. He waits to see if I've got anything more to say before he speaks again.

"What I did, keeping Freya's death from you, it was selfish."

"No, you were trying to protect me."

"I should have told you."

"But I understand why you didn't. I do. When I found out she was gone … I needed someone to blame and not just Juliette or the vampires. I needed someone I could take my anger out on in person. And it shouldn't have been you. You just became the whipping boy."

"I deserved it."

"No." I shrug. "Well, maybe a little but not the way I've

behaved recently. I've just been cruel. You enabled Oliver to rescue me from Scotland. You were the one who brought the wolves to save us in Lithuania. You found us a safe place to stay in France, at Régine's. You've done so much for me, and I'm truly sorry."

"Narissa, you have nothing to apologise for."

"That's not true. You've given up a way of life for me. I just hope that, with a bit of time, we can get things back to normal. Whatever that means for us."

There's a tension here now, but different to recently. It's causing an ache to spread through me. What is normal for Calin and me? Is it more than just ripping each other's clothes off in a wooden cabin?

"You should forgive Oliver, too, you know."

His words banish those images in a flash and cause me to snort, half in anger, half in disgust.

"Oliver is a totally different situation."

"He was just trying to protect me."

"He was trying to protect himself. Once I knew the truth, there was no reason not to come clean. He watched me berate you. Watched me hate you. And all the time he knew he was no different."

My mind goes back where I don't want it to. Oliver kissing me. His lips against my ear, whispering insincere words of love. Calin never pretended like that.

"Let's not talk about him," I say quietly.

"Okay."

Silence falls on us and I want to stretch across and hold his hand. As if he can read my mind, he tentatively reaches out, not to touch my hand, just to place his there between us, within my grasp.

"I've missed you," he says.

"I've missed you."

And then, feeling more tired than I've been in days, I shift next to him, taking his hand and wrapping his arm around my neck. I lay my head against his shoulder … and fall asleep.

29

When I wake up, the car is rumbling down the ramp and off the ferry into the fading light of the port. Dover, England. I'm in the same position I fell asleep in, next to Calin in the middle of the back seat. Esther is now on my opposite side. Guilt sparks in me as I realise that the fact I've slept the entire journey means Calin hasn't had a chance to move the whole time.

"Sorry," I say to him. "You should have woken me."

"It's fine. The crossing wasn't long, and I've done it enough times not to be interested in the view."

When I turn the other way, a knowing twinkle sparkles in Esther's eye. I quickly look out of the window.

"As soon as we're through the port, we start the plan, which means I'll need to leave you and head to London by myself," Rhett says.

"Are we sure this is the best course of action?" I ask, sensing that he's been waiting for me to wake up before announcing this. "You said that Vasara's spell will cover all our scents. It seems silly to go separately to the same place."

"He'll expect me to arrive on foot. And she can only cover the scent of living things, remember. Not petrol fumes and leather upholstery. It's fine, we know what we're doing. There's no need to rendezvous again. Just remember, don't go in until you see me come and stand at the window."

"What if he doesn't take you into the Council meeting room? What if he wants to go somewhere else?"

A small smile, that I've grown rather fond of, curls on Rhett's lips.

"Trust me, if I tell him that's where I want us to talk, that's where we'll be."

It's only one less person in the car, yet immediately it feels a lot emptier. And quieter.

We dropped Rhett off in a layby less than five miles from the ferry, at which point Esther moved into the front seat, next to Vasara. Calin offered, but I sense that, no matter how much Vasara trusts Rhett, she can't yet extend the same goodwill to all vampires and having a wolf next to her for the rest of the journey makes her feel a little less uneasy. And so, it's me and Calin alone in the back seat again.

For the next two or three miles, no one speaks. The sound of cars racing by is the only thing that filters through the windows. I wonder how easy it will be for Rhett to find his way. After all, if he doesn't come to England that often, it's probably changed a lot since the last time he was here. But he's a big boy and it's dark. I'm sure he'll be fine. If he isn't, then we're all screwed.

"When were you last over here?" I ask Vasara.

"Me? Oh, I've never been before."

Her answer catches me by surprise.

"You haven't? But your English is perfect."

"Three of us are from here. We also have one who's Welsh. I feel it's important to be able to speak in all the mother tongues of my coven."

"Wow, how many languages is that?" I ask.

"At last count, nine."

"Nine!"

That might even put Oliver to shame. At some point, I'll have to tell him. Knowing his competitive streak, he'll make it his business to go out and learn some more.

"You know, I've never been to England, either," Esther says, from the front seat.

"What?"

This comment surprises me almost as much as Vasara's knowledge of languages.

"Not once?"

"Nope. It was an unspoken rule. South Pack stayed down here. We stayed up there, in Scotland. And both avoided the vampires at all costs. That was the deal, before Juliette went crazy, that is."

"But you went to Italy on your honeymoon."

"We flew from Glasgow. And when I fled the pack, I got

a boat across to Holland. So, this'll be my first time in England, too."

"Wow, two people who've never been here before. No pressure or anything then."

We chuckle light-heartedly, but it doesn't disguise the tension that's rippling beneath the surface. No pressure? Of course there's pressure. This must work, not just for Rey's sake but for all of us.

There's a niggling in the pit of my stomach. One that's been there since we devised this plan, and it's still not gone away. It's a point we've discussed over and over, to the extent that I'm certain the others are sick of me mentioning it. But the closer to London we get, it bothers me more and I need to check just one last time. I turn to Calin.

"I'm worried about Polidori knowing you're there. Being able catch your scent."

Vasara is the one who replies.

"I'll do the best for him I can," she says and for not the first time.

"But you've said yourself that the spell doesn't work well on non-living things."

"We don't need to worry about it," Calin says.

He takes my hand in a way that was, for a short while, so natural. I feel my breath hitch. I think he's going to let go of me, but he doesn't.

"My scent is already all over the Vampire Council building. It's been there for years. Vasara will weaken anything I leave behind on this visit. That will be enough to make it appear old.

Besides, we're not going anywhere near the Council rooms where Rhett and Polidori will be. The vault is next to the dungeons. Hearing us is more of a concern than him smelling me, and you're not worried about that because you know Rhett will deal with it. You just have to trust me. Can you do that?"

His eyes lock on mine and it feels like it's just the two of us again, and we're back in the little hut in the forest outside my mother's wolf camp.

"Yes," I say. "I trust you."

"Good." He gives me a small smile. "Then let's go get these grimoires."

30

Rhett

It is safe to say that I'm outside my comfort zone. It's partly being in London and near so many people. I do like humans, far more than my own kind, in fact. But being around them evokes memories of my original life and family, then how I was forced to live after I was first turned, when people were treated as food, as commodities and nothing more. It's hard to see them jam-packed on the underground these days and not think of the way we used to cram them into cages, their lives only valued by the volume of blood they contained.

Centuries may have passed, yet the sights and sounds remain as clear to me as yesterday. I shudder as I recall the massacres. Sometimes, we would raid an entire village. We'd enter in the dead of night and pull everyone we could find from their beds, whether young, old, male, female, strong or infirm. We'd drag them away kicking and screaming and shove them into wagons, where they would huddle together, weeping, the stench of human soil ripe in the air. We'd sometimes drive for days until we reached the castle again. Some of them wouldn't survive the journey, but those who did, arrived limp, weakened by dehydration and starvation. That was the way the Duchess liked them, the blood in their veins thick and viscous. We were then allowed to eat but only at her discretion.

Eve arrived in such a wagon. Eve, who changed everything. She was not brought to be fed from; she was brought to be tested on, to endure suffering and torture that no one should ever have to bear. Even now, I often find myself wondering what would have happened if she hadn't come that night, if she hadn't spoken to me. Would my humanity have eventually slipped away as it did for so many of my kind? Would I, too, have come to believe I was better than all of those with a pulse? As much as I like to think otherwise, I know the truth. She was the one who saved me. She was the one who saw that slight glimmer of compassion before it was extinguished, and she was the one who made me fight to keep it.

Would she be proud of me now for what I'm trying to do? Would she recognise my attempt at redemption? I suspect not. She hoped for so much more from me, and whatever these wolves might think, I let her down. But I keep trying to make amends. And I've got plenty of time.

I keep to backstreets as I move quickly through the darkened city. Then I cross the river. I've been here a few

CHAPTER 30

times before, and although a lot has changed, my feet seem to recall the way. It sounds like a cliché to say I'm drawn to the place. I'm not. I simply want to get there as fast as possible.

It's an impressive building, with its gothic columns and ornate arches. I wonder how many of the vampires who use it know the true reason for its construction. I don't doubt Polidori does, but the others, I suspect, are all too young.

It was built for vampires. In that sense, its purpose has not changed greatly, only its facade. The dungeons were for storing humans then, not wayward vampires. The Council rooms themselves were dining halls for parties, night-long orgies, which so many people attended, but few ever left. Maybe that's why I've never believed Polidori's agenda. Why set up shop in a place with echoes of such horror? Why preach peace in a place where dried blood must line the joints of the slate flooring? Maybe he thinks it's a way of atoning for the past, of converting a place of terror into one of peace. I doubt it.

Before I've even reached the door, I know that he's done as I asked. The place is empty. The stench of vampire still swirls thickly in the air, but there's not a footstep to be heard inside. Not a creaking floorboard. Not at the lower levels, at least. Up at the top, I'm not so sure. There's certainly some movement there. Knowing Polidori, he's probably got fresh food in for the occasion. There certainly doesn't sound much to worry about.

I take my phone out of my pocket to check the time. No communication. That was what we agreed. Timing is crucial. I've got another four minutes to wait before I head inside. Then, if everything goes to plan, the others will enter shortly after.

I'm tense, and that's something I haven't felt in a very long time. This is the right thing to do, I remind myself. This is what needs to happen.

The minutes tick by, and when it finally hits nine p.m., I slip my phone back into my pocket and walk to the entrance.

So, this is it. This is where I put on the best performance of my life.

31

Narissa

We park up over a mile away from the Council building. None of us says a word as we quickly start making our way there. I check my watch. Rhett should be in by now. We must arrive in time for his signal.

Once we're in, we'll have no way of knowing how long it will take us to find the grimoires. Calin has a good idea where in the vault they might be kept but cannot be certain. Rhett will do his best to keep Polidori busy in conversation for as long as possible and hope he doesn't get suspicious. But time is a luxury we don't have, and one wrong word could see Polidori throwing him out or, worse still, asking other vampires to join them.

A stupid joke floats into my head. *A vampire, a witch and two werewolves walk into a bar* … It's not even a joke and there's no punchline I can think of. Maybe just the four of us here, thinking we're going to pull off this heist, is where the real joke lies.

I'm so lost in my daydream that I don't hear the late-night cyclist's bell ringing behind me. Not until he's right up to me and shouting, do I realise the focus of his anger is me.

"Get out of the way!" he yells, offering me the middle finger as I step back.

I hadn't even noticed I was on a cycle path, and from the shocked looks of the others, they too were lost in their own thoughts and hadn't realised, either.

"Try not to get yourself injured," Vasara says, as we continue on. "Remember, we're all under the same cloaking spell. If one of us gets hurt, then all of us do."

I briefly think about the logistics of what she's telling me before voicing my opinion on the matter.

"That seems ridiculous. Grouping everyone together like that. Accidents—or worse—can happen. Surely it's dangerous?"

"I agree it's less than ideal," she says, shifting her rucksack a little higher as it starts to slip down.

It's apparently filled with various witch paraphernalia: candles, herbs and that sort of thing. The rest of us are also carrying rucksacks, but ours are empty. Hopefully, they will soon be stuffed full of grimoires.

"So why is it like that?"

"Lack of skill, pure and simple. Like I said, everything we know has been pieced together through trial and error.

There are many gaps in our knowledge that we hope to rectify after today."

"As long as one of us doesn't get knocked over by a bike first," Esther says, helpfully, from behind me.

I offer her my best Alpha glare, although it has little effect on her smirk.

It's so strange being back in London. Everything looks the same, from shops laden with tourist tat—I ♥ London T-shirts and Big Ben snow globes—to the endless traffic choking up the roads, even at this late hour. Groups of men and women, dressed up to the nines, laugh as they stagger to yet another bar. There are couples, some walking hand in hand, others bickering as they go. None of this has changed yet it feels different. I'm not the same person anymore. Part of me wants to talk to the others to ease my sense of foreboding, but I don't. I keep my thoughts to myself.

We're almost at the Vampire Council head-quarters. *The Vampire Council.* I let the words swirl around my mind. We're going to break into the Vampire Council. I'm going to put myself in the same building as Polidori. The thought would have always been terrifying, but now I've seen what Rhett is capable of, I can't help but wonder how powerful he is, too. Hopefully, it's something I won't have to find out.

A deep dread is roiling around in my stomach. This doesn't feel good. Part of me wants to call the whole thing off, but when has my gut instinct ever been right? Maybe it's a good thing. Perhaps a bit of fear will keep me on my toes.

We come to a stop in a small park across from the

building. We're standing unusually close, but I'd rather that than be on my own right now.

"Is he inside?" I ask Calin. "Can you hear them?"

He lifts his head and cocks it to one side.

"He is. They're talking."

"Anyone else?"

He frowns, a small wrinkle creasing his brow. My heart rate rises.

"What is it?" I ask. "Who else is there?"

"Humans."

"Humans?" I say. "Why would humans be there?"

The question has barely left my lips when I realise the answer. They are there as refreshments. I shudder. Perhaps they've come from Blackwatch. Maybe they at least have an inkling of what they've signed up for. The most I can hope is that, with Rhett there, things won't go too far, but he'll need to do whatever it takes to keep us safe long enough to get those grimoires. I can't dwell on this. I have to think of Rey.

"Which room is it?" I ask Calin.

"Third floor, second from the corner."

Just as he says this, the heavy curtains move and are then drawn open. Rhett stands there, framed by the tall window.

"Okay then, let's do it," I say, pushing the notion of human snacks to the back of my mind. Let's get inside this place. Let's get those grimoires."

32

Rhett

"I do so love a cityscape by night," I say.

I gaze out, as if admiring the distant view. In reality I'm looking far closer to home, for signs of Vasara and the others.

"Don't get me wrong, I'm very fond of my little place in the country, but a city holds so many ..." I see them make their move from the shadows. "... possibilities."

"Yes, indeed. But I must admit, given the way our last conversation ended, I was most surprised to hear from you. You seemed adamant you wanted to continue with your life of seclusion."

He sits in a prepossessing chair, in what I assume is his customary place at the head of the vast table, his hands on the armrests as he leans back. It's common knowledge that vampires don't age, but that doesn't mean they don't change. His eyes have sunk deeper. A permanent sneer plays on his lips.

"I realised that I may have been a little hasty," I say. "The least I should have done was hear you out. The reception you received was not, how shall I put it …?"

"Polite?"

"Perhaps."

When you've lived as long as I have, you become very good at reading people, and while I'm far from being a social butterfly, even a recluse like me meets his fair share of folk. Believe me when I say I've seen them all: the liars and the cheats, the do-gooders and the philanthropists, the con men and the saints. This fellow behaves like the worst of them, including the arrogant way he looks down his nose at me. He's always treated others with conceit, as if no one could possibly better him, but I'll be honest, it's not what I expected tonight. I'm not saying I require homage, but a little deference wouldn't be out of place. I'm the elder here by a considerable number of years. Rather than showing a modicum of respect, he seems almost amused by my presence here.

"How rude of me," he says, standing up. "I haven't offered you anything to drink. Let me rectify that."

He reaches for a small brass bell on the table and rings it. At once, the door to the left of me opens and a dozen people are herded in. Men and women alike, they're dressed in skimpy clothing, little more than underwear. Goosebumps cover their skin as they react to a chill we don't feel. A full spectrum of the human race is on offer:

white, black, Asian, Latino, red heads and blondes. A veritable smorgasbord.

I'd heard that Blackwatch provides only volunteers, who are happy with the terms they're offered, usually involving large sums of money, but these people definitely don't look willing. There are marks on their arms where they've already been repeatedly fed from, or it might be more accurate to say overfed from. Several of them seem to be wearing thickly applied make-up which is no doubt disguising bruises beneath.

"I'm afraid I couldn't quite remember what your preferences were," Polidori says, "so I ordered a selection."

"Willing ones?" I ask, making no attempt to hide my look of disgust. "Thank you for the offer, but I ate before I came."

He inhales sharply through his nose and seems to be working hard to keep his composure. With a flick of a hand, he waves them away.

"Don't go far," he tells them, as they shuffle hurriedly out.

He sits down again.

"Well then, as you're the one who has come to me, why don't you tell me what has brought you here?"

"I thought I made myself clear. I wanted to apologise for my hasty reaction the last time we spoke. I realise I was … abrupt."

"An apology can be sent by post. Or a telephone call would have sufficed. Maybe even an email if that quaint cottage of yours has Wi-Fi."

He smirks at his own little joke.

"You can't tell me you've abandoned your solitary lifestyle and travelled all this way, simply to say sorry."

His eyes bore into me. It's an intimidation technique I expect works well on younger vampires, perhaps even on members of his Council, but I am neither. I stare back with equal steeliness before remembering why I *am* here. This is not about my sensibilities. It's not about how much this creature repulses me to my very core. It's about getting the others enough time to retrieve the grimoires. It's about keeping Vasara safe, so that she can find what she needs.

"You said change will be coming," I say. "That we will not have to hide any more. For someone who has lived as a recluse as I have, as you so bluntly put it, this intrigues me. Upon reflection, maybe it is something I would be interested in. Perhaps you'd be good enough to elaborate for me. How do you see it working, and how do you think the humans will respond?"

He smiles, displaying his glistening fangs. How many humans have those bottom ones turned? I wonder. Probably so many, before he started wearing this patina of restraint and compassion, that even he's lost count. My tongue finds my own fangs and moves gently across them. It's easy for me to remember how many I've been responsible for. Zero. Not one. Not even when Eve begged me to save her dying child. That, at least, is one thing I'll admit the Council has got right—removing lower fangs to stop the turnings—even if it is under the false narrative of protection, as opposed to the truth: preserving power for the few. But isn't that what politics has always been about, when you get to the heart of it?

CHAPTER 32

"Humans, as you know, are fickle creatures," Polidori starts. "For all their talk of morality, their inconsistencies are more numerous than there are waves on the oceans. Some of them worship cows, while others eat them. Some of them work to preserve the forests, while others hack them down. Some spend billions on space exploration, while their countrymen starve. There is no rhyme or reason to the way they behave.

"For years, I have watched their development, and with each leap in technology, I've hoped they would find a way to live in harmony. I've tried to work with them, to subtly guide them, searching for a commonality to bring them together, a thread of, dare I say it, humanity to unite them. But I can no longer waste my time looking for something that will never be there. They are hell-bent on self-destruction, and they will take us with them. As such, my concern is no longer for them. It is for us. They've had their chance and now it is time to subjugate them."

He leans forwards and steeples his hands together.

"I see you are not quite convinced. Perhaps it would be better if you heard more of my vision from someone else. It would help you realise I'm not alone in my thinking."

Reaching into his jacket, Polidori retrieves his phone. He taps on the screen before putting the device aside. He's messaged someone but who? Who on earth could he possibly imagine I would listen to?

"He'll just be a moment," he says.

For a reason I can't fathom, a chill runs down my spine. Chills aren't something a vampire encounters that often, certainly not onc with my experience. Yet, right now, I feel remarkably akin to those humans he displayed only a few minutes ago. I sense something is coming. I just don't know what it is. That's when I catch a scent I haven't smelt for hundreds of years drifting up from the floor below. My unease grows tenfold as a smile blooms on Polidori's face. The footsteps draw closer. Someone is coming up the staircase and along the corridor. As they reach the door, I try to keep my composure. I try not to show the fear that is rolling through me in waves.

"Let me introduce you to the newest member of the Vampire Council," Polidori says, eyes shining. "I believe you two already know each other."

33

Narissa

Vasara stays next to Calin. Esther and I follow behind. The scent cloaking will work best if we stay in close proximity, Vasara said. Since Calin's is the most difficult to mask, she wants him closest to her. Right now, I'm happy to do whatever she says. I don't think I could give any orders, even if I wanted to. For some reason, being in charge when I'm a wolf is infinitely easier than when I'm human. There's a confidence then that I'm not currently experiencing. And all my failures have happened in this city. All the shit that screwed up my life, started here. It's easy to get lost in these thoughts, but I have to shrug them away. This is for Rey. I can do this for her.

Next to me, Esther is unusually quiet. Her eyes go back and forth as she places each foot carefully, focusing on remaining silent. I watch her swallowing repeatedly. If she's scared, that isn't a good sign, but I'm infinitely thankful now that Lou suggested I bring a wolf with me. I'm not sure how I could have done this solo, walking behind Calin and Vasara with no one beside me. If it wasn't the most un-alpha thing to do, I would hold her hand.

We pass along one corridor and then another. High ceilings and dark wood surround us. Gothic archways with ornate carvings. It's possible I've been through here before, either unconscious or as a wolf, but understandably, I don't recognise it. Calin stops as we reach a sturdy looking oak door with thick metal hinges and an elaborate lock the size of a brick. I'm hoping this isn't where we're going. Breaking down something this massive wouldn't be a good way of staying inconspicuous. Without a word, he points to the door and looks at Vasara. She nods, apparently understanding what he's saying without a single word spoken.

Stepping forwards, she searches in her bag, then brings out two small vials of powder. She unscrews the lids and mouths something silently, before flicking their contents onto the hinges, the lock and the handle. Static buzzes through the air. She steps back, looks at Calin and nods. He now moves forwards and twists the handle. The door opens with an eerie silence, not just quietly but with an absolute absence of sound.

Esther and I exchange glances.

"Wow," she mouths to me.

Calin now nods at us. Through the door—of all the things I didn't want to see—is a staircase leading down into darkness. Fucking stairs and fucking dungeon-type

CHAPTER 33

places! Cellars and old docks. I get it, vampires don't like daylight. They need dark places, but for once, wouldn't it be possible to have something happen above ground? Taking a deep breath, I follow Calin and Vasara as they descend.

It's pitch black, which is probably fine for the vampires who normally come here, but within four steps, I can no longer see.

"Vasara," I whisper.

"I'm on it. *Sviesa*."

It's not like in the movies. There's no massive, glowing sphere bobbing along in front of us, there's just a steady light, dim but somehow natural, just enough for us to see the steps and not stumble.

When we reach the last one, corridors split off in three directions: straight ahead, left and right. As much as I was apprehensive about Calin coming with us, I know now we'd have had no chance of finding our way without him.

"We should be okay to talk down here," he says, in little more than a whisper. "Quietly at least. These walls are well reinforced. The vampires don't like it when sounds from the dungeons reach the upper rooms. But we should keep it to a minimum, all the same. Just what needs to be said."

"Okay. Which way now?" I ask.

"The vault is just up here."

I slip next to Calin.

"You okay?" he asks me.

"Ask me again when we're back in the car."

"I will. And don't worry, we'll be out of here soon."

Just up here, as Calin put it, is a minute's walk. There's no way we can still be under the same building. Either that, or I really didn't appreciate the size of it from the outside.

"This is us. This is the vault."

I'm not sure I would have spotted it, had he not pointed it out, especially considering I was looking for a door with a lock, like the one upstairs. This is merely an archway. No door. No shielding. Just a gap in the wall that leads into a large room beyond.

"I expected more security," I say.

"I don't think you have to worry about locks when you're a vampire," Esther says. "Besides, there'd be guards upstairs normally, wouldn't there?"

"True," I say, before looking at Vasara. "Over to you now. Can you find what we need?"

A small smile creeps onto the older woman's face.

"I'd say it was a job I was born to do."

Calin is the first to step through into the vault. I guess it's pretty much what I was expecting: dark, gloomy and immense. What seems like miles and miles of racks stretch away from us under the brick arches.

"Don't touch anything," Calin says, as I flip up the lid of a small wooden box on the first set of shelves.

I offer him my best grimace, at which he shakes his head, half amused. I guess he already knew I'd be straight in. Given that the box is already open, it seems silly not to look inside, although the moment I do, I regret it. Two severed fingertips lie on a red velvet cushion, the nails and skin purply black. Shards of bone protrude from the ends. Bile burns the back of my throat.

"Trust me, there's a lot worse in here than that," he

CHAPTER 33

says, coming up beside me and pushing the lid down. "Better just stay by me and let Vasara do her thing."

It's then that I see she's still standing by the entrance. She closes her eyes and holds out her hands.

Her eyes snap open.

"The grimoires are deeper in," she says. "Follow me."

We do. There are no lights, or if there are, Calin is not going to risk using them, and the glow around Vasara continues to be our only illumination. It appears to be dimmer than it was on the staircase. Perhaps some of her power is being used in another direction, searching for the books.

"This way," she says, and takes a left turn. The aisle is narrower here as shelves are replaced by large crates. Great wooden boxes. Trunks, like the type you'd store blankets in or pack your child off to boarding school with, if you were that way inclined. She slows, coming to a stop about halfway along this section.

"These are all grimoires," she says, pointing to the boxes. "All the witches' knowledge. Centuries of it. All buried here. I can feel the power and the energy."

She stops and frowns.

"And darkness."

Whether it's my imagination or not, I understand what she's sensing. It's almost as if the boxes are vibrating with potential.

"How will you know which is the right one, which one contains a spell to save Rey?" I ask.

She presses her lips together, which is not the response I was after.

"I can make an educated guess. I can tell the white magic from the black, but there might be another way to show us which grimoires are the most powerful. They're the ones we want."

From a pocket, she retrieves a small bag and empties the contents into her left hand. They seem to be seeds, just like when she visited Rey, although rather than keeping a single one on her palm, she leaves the entire packet.

"Do you always have those on you?" I ask, unable to stop myself. I know I've had the habit of keeping random stuff in my pockets over the years—hair ties, pens, even bottle tops—but never seeds.

"Our magic comes from the earth," she answers and sprinkles them over the crates. "It is gifted to us. It's useful to keep a little bit of nature to hand, just in case."

"Like an energy bar for magic," I say, then immediately regret it when both Calin and Esther offer me their most withering looks. I feel my cheeks colour. Apparently, being the Alpha doesn't put me above making stupid comments.

"I suppose it is a bit like that," she says, then closes her eyes and holds out her hands.

She starts to utter a spell I immediately recognise. It's the same one she used to make the plant grow in the old coal store, but something quite different happens here. All the seeds sprout at the same moment, shoots stretching upwards and forming their first leaves. That's when things change. Many continue to grow like the first time, steadily, sturdily upwards. But others are racing away in every direction, like vines. Before I can even blink, they're producing flowers, some of which turn black the moment they've formed. The stems carry on growing, but the petals of affected flowers curl in on themselves, shrivelling as if they've been caught in a flame. It's incredible to watch, like a time-lapse recording of the death of a thousand roses, while the aroma of the surviving ones fills the air.

Vasara drops her hands, and it all stops.

We're left with what looks like part of an abandoned mansion, where nature has been left to run wild. Some of the crates are barely visible now, they're covered in so many blooms. Others are hidden by sooty petals.

"Don't go near those," Vasara says, pointing at the crates covered in the blackened flowers. "They're contain black magic. Look for the ones where the flowers are healthy and large. Those contain the strongest white magic. They're the ones we want."

Three of the vines have grown far and away the strongest and most abundant flowers of those still thriving. Calin uses his vampire strength to rip the lids off the boxes they're wrapped around. Vasara sorts through the contents and identifies a total of ten grimoires for us to take, ten massive books that we need to get out of here.

"I guess this is where I make myself useful," Esther says, bending down and picking one up. "Jeez, these things are heavy."

I follow suit and discover she's right, they're as heavy as hell. We take off our rucksacks and carefully put the tomes in, then reach for more. After three, I tentatively test the weight of my bag.

"I'm not sure I can even get these back upstairs, let alone make it all the way to the car," I mutter.

"Here," says Vasara, rubbing her hands over my pack, intoning quietly as she does so.

"That should help," she says, indicating for me to try again, "although this spell will wear off quickly. Just let me know when it starts to feel too heavy again, and I'll reinforce it."

I hoist my bag up onto my shoulder and if feels significantly lighter. Vasara goes through the same procedure with Esther's, before moving on to Calin who, despite having four in his pack, shakes his head.

"It's not a problem. Save your power for something else," he says.

"I could have done with you when I was carting books around at uni and doing my back in every day," I say to Vasara, who laughs.

"Okay, let's get out of here," Esther says. "This is not a place I want to hang around in."

"I second that," I say, before my thoughts shift. "How do you think Rhett is getting on? Do you think he's convinced Polidori he wants to join forces with him?"

"As long as he's keeping him busy, that's all that matters," Calin says, striding back to the entrance.

"As long as he is safe," Vasara counters.

Now that we've got the grimoires, there's a new sense of urgency, and I realise part of me thought we wouldn't make it this far, that we'd fall at the first hurdle, whatever that was. But we haven't. We've got them, and tomorrow, when we return to France, I'm going to get Rey back, too.

"I think we're going to need a bit more illumination

going up," Esther says. "I don't fancy my chances of carrying these things if I can't see the steps properly."

"You might have to just do your best," Vasara says. "Keeping Calin's scent shrouded and the weight of your packs down would be manageable in any other situation. But this place, with its undercurrent of death, is drawing on my power far more than I feared it would. I'll do what I can, but it might not be easy going."

"It'll be okay," I say, recognising that she feels she's letting us down. "This is amazing. What you've done is unbelievable. Calin can guide us, can't you?"

"Of course," he replies.

"You just do what you can, Vasara."

Once again in the lead, Calin steps out of the vault and into the corridor. As I'm about to follow, Vasara's light dims, flickering like a candle that's nearly spent.

"Stop!" she yells, grabbing me from behind and yanking me away from the opening. The weight of the books on my back pulls me off balance and I topple against a shelf, sending boxes crashing to the ground in a cacophony of unwelcome noise.

Calin spins around.

"What was that all about?" Esther snaps. "Polidori must have heard that din. We've really got to shift it, now."

She goes to follow Calin.

"Wait!" Vasara shouts with such urgency it stops Esther in her tracks.

Once again, she reaches into her pocket for seeds, this time selecting only one and placing it on her palm. She lets it grow just until the first bud has formed, then pulls back her arm and throws it through the entrance.

"What the—" Esther starts, but her words are stolen by what happens next. The previously healthy plant withers and crumples the instant it passes through the opening and what lands on the floor at Calin's feet, is nothing more than a pile of dust. My blood turns to ice.

"Egress has been blocked by an ancient curse more powerful than anything I've encountered before."

"What does that mean?" I ask.

"It means that no living thing can leave," she replies. "We're trapped."

34

Rhett

"Rhett."

"Dimitar?"

"It's been a long time."

"Yes, it has. What would it be, two hundred years? Three hundred?"

"I believe the last time I saw you was at the Duchess's castle." He smiles. "The night of the escape, if I recall correctly."

"Was it really that long ago?"

I try to sound casual, like I can hardly remember, but he knows exactly when it was. I can see from the glint in his eyes. Dimitar is everything I hate in my kind. Vicious, cruel, sadistic. If he'd had his way, humans would be kept in cages, bought and sold like cattle. In truth, I thought he'd perished long ago, around the time when the Blood Pact came into force. But perhaps that was more hope that belief.

"So, you've crawled out from under your rock," he says, with a smirk. "You know, I heard some very peculiar rumours about you last century, that you were running with witches. But that can't be right, can it?"

"I thought you destroyed every witch. And every werewolf, too. Wasn't that what you told people you were going to do? And if we're talking about disappointingly untrue rumours, I heard that you'd been staked by a monk in Florence, over a century ago."

Polidori steps between us, resting a hand on our shoulders.

"Now, now, gentlemen, let's play nicely, shall we? After all, you're both here as my guests."

"Just a guest, Polidori?" Dimitar says, looking at me. "I assumed I became more than that when I accepted a seat on your Council."

"You're on the Council?" I ask. "That's an interesting development. Then I guess our days of keeping peace with humans really are over."

"What can I say? Polidori wished to liven things up a bit. And there's nothing like experience to achieve that."

"So that's it? Vampires out in the open for all the world to see? That's the plan?"

"That's the short version, I suppose," Polidori says. "You won't mind if we don't indulge you with all the details just yet, will you?"

If I hadn't been feeling sick before, I am now. Humans

outnumber vampires by vast numbers. They always have. Hundreds of thousands of humans to each vampire. If they wanted us dead, even our strength and feeding habits wouldn't be enough to overcome their military power. Unless … unless Polidori has already considered this.

"I assume you have people in high places to help you succeed with this. Human help."

"The very highest of places, in fact. Although they will not remain human, of course. One of their conditions, you understand."

"And vampire numbers?"

"Have been significantly underestimated in the last hundred years but particularly so in the last decade."

"You've been turning more?"

The broad smile on his face says it all. Shit. The arrogance. No wonder people imagine us to be monsters. Beside me, Dimitar is wearing a close-lipped sneer. If I were to hazard a guess, I'd say he's played a vital role in turning as many humans as possible. Not to mention *persuading* those in authority to side with their cause.

"How many?" I ask, trying to keep my tone indifferent.

Polidori continues to smile.

"Come now, you can't think I'm going to let you in on all our secrets just like that. Not when you've been away for so long. Not when you've been keeping such questionable company over the years."

I'm sick of their gloating. I want to leave, but I must give the others more time.

"Questionable company? You're taking Dimitar's word on this?"

"I don't take anyone's word without evidence, but I have other sources and ways of discovering who is telling the truth. All I'm asking of you is your assurance that, when the time comes, you'll be on our side. I can assure you the rewards will be plentiful."

There's something about the way he's talking, the way he said that last line. It's as if I'm not the first one to have heard that little speech.

Dimitar's eyes have narrowed on me, like he's trying to see inside my mind. There was a time when I was frightened of him, fearful of the things he could do, but those days are gone. He's only survived by being a relentless bully. But I can give as good as I get, nowadays.

"So, what do you want from me," I ask, ignoring his stare and focusing on Polidori. "How can I assure you of my commitment?"

"Funny you should ask," he replies.

35

Narissa

In my defence, I thought the way things were going was too good to be true, but this ... this is something I had never considered.

"What do you mean, no living thing can leave?"

"It's exactly what I've said. If we were to attempt to pass through that archway, we would end up the same as the plant."

"As dust?" Esther clarifies.

"I believe so."

We're stunned to silence. Calin is looking at me.

"But Calin ..." I say, realising the answer to my question before I've even finished it.

"Calin isn't living. It's the perfect setup. No need for

guards. Only vampires can come and go. Anyone else becomes trapped."

"Or else dies trying to leave," I say.

"Exactly."

"Narissa," Calin begins, fear etched on his face, "I didn't know."

"You wouldn't," Vasara replies. "I suspect very few are even aware of the curse and secrecy is what makes it so effective."

For a while the only sounds are the breaths quivering from our lungs. Vasara stretches her hand out and steps towards the door. Once again, the light around her dims and flickers the closer she gets, which must have been what alerted her to the danger in the first place.

"Hold on," I say, dropping my bag on the floor. "It's a spell, right?"

"Yes. A very strong one," she replies. "As I said, it feels like it's been in place for centuries."

"So, it must have been put in place by a witch. Can't you undo it?"

She looks down at the grimoires poking out of my backpack.

"It's ancient and powerful magic … maybe, if I had enough time, I could find something in those that might work."

"Well, we're not going anywhere," I say. "Tell us what we're looking for."

I tip the grimoires out onto the floor.

Vasara pinches the bridge of her nose.

"I don't suppose any of you can read Lithuanian?"

"No," we say in unison.

I decide that, when I get my arse back into gear, I'll learn a second language and Lithuanian is going to be my number-one choice.

"Okay then. We need to find something that looks like one of these."

Using a finger, she etches two patterns in the dust on the floor. The first one is circular, almost like a wheel, but rather than straight spokes, the sections are separated by curved lines. The second one comprises three interlinked circles with triangles sitting on top of each.

"Be gentle with the pages. After all these years, they'll be very delicate and so will the ink. Turn them by their corners, so as not to damage any of the spells."

She pulls a grimoire from my bag, opens it and scans down the first page, before turning carefully to the next and then the next.

"I think damaging the spells is the least of our problems right now," Esther mutters, although she says it quietly enough that Vasara doesn't hear her.

Stepping back through the entrance, Calin pulls out the books he's been carrying, places them on the ground next to me and starts searching with the rest of us.

"I'm sorry, I should have known," he says.

"Why would you?" I reply. "This is not your fault. Don't worry, we'll find the spell we need, and we'll all get out of here in one piece."

My confidence is still fairly strong as I reach the end of my first grimoire. There are plenty more to go. But as we each reach yet another back page without finding anything, my nerves start to jangle.

"Are these definitely the right ones?" I ask Vasara. "Are you sure that what we need couldn't be in any of the others?"

"To allow someone to travel in one direction but not the other, would involve an incredibly sophisticated and complicated spell. One like that would almost certainly be written down, and these contain the strongest in here. Except …"

She pauses. Her eyes darken. An idea manifests itself in my mind before she can give voice to it. So, I say it for her.

"The grimoires of black magic?"

"I should have thought of it before. The countermeasure for a curse might only exist alongside the original instructions. If that's not it, then I don't know what else we can try to bring it down."

"It's not like we have much choice, is it?" Esther says.

We move silently back to the area of the vault housing the grimoires. There we find half a dozen containers which appear to be likely contenders, judging by the number of burnt flowers around them. However, one stands out from the rest. A blackened plant has continued to grow on it, even in the absence of Vasara's magic. It has twisted itself around it with such force that the crate has burst open. One of the books, in particular, seems to have been singled out and is warping under the pressure of the constricting vines.

Without a word, Vasara reaches down, rips off the blackened stems and picks it up. Kneeling on the ground, she touches only the very edges of the pages as she turns them, as if to do any more than that might allow the black magic to seep into her skin.

None of us moves. I try to steady my breathing to make as little noise as possible, which is hard as my heart is hammering away loud enough to drown out a steel band.

"She's going to find it," Esther says, taking my hand and squeezing it. "Don't worry. She's got this."

A moment later, a small gasp escapes from Vasara's lips.

"What is it? Have you found it?" I ask. "Do you know how to break the spell?"

She pauses, for so long I think she hasn't heard my question. But as I go to repeat it, she answers me, although her voice is barely a whisper.

"I know what we have to do."

Relief floods through me and I grin at Esther. But when I look at Calin, I find his brow is furrowed in concern. Turning back to Vasara, I see that her hands are shaking violently.

"What is it?" I ask. "What does it involve?"

She goes to speak but fails. It's only when she clears her throat and tries for a second time, that she manages to get her words out.

"A sacrifice," she says. "To break the spell, requires a blood sacrifice."

36

The silence swallows us whole. No one speaks. No one questions her. But neither does anyone want to believe what they've heard is true.

The seconds tick by, and they're all looking at me. Esther waits for her Alpha's response. For Vasara, I'm the one who brought her here to save my friend, for whom three of us are now going to die. Calin just looks horrified.

"No," I shake my head, "that can't happen. There has to be another way. Try another grimoire. There were plenty more with white magic spells, that we didn't take. The one we need could be in one of those."

"It won't be," Vasara says, matter-of factly but not unkindly. "These are the strongest in the vault. You saw that."

"Then we try somewhere else. Maybe there's another room, behind a secret door, perhaps. Calin? Could you go and look? There might be even more powerful grimoires elsewhere. We just need to keep searching."

I twist around, heart racing. I'm panicking now and press my hands against the nearest wall, pushing like it might give way and reveal a hidden escape route.

"There must be somewhere else. There has to be."

I'm speaking more to myself than anyone else, trying to stop the voice whirring around in my head, telling me this is hopeless. As I turn to back to the others, Calin catches my hand.

"There's nowhere else, Narissa."

"I don't believe that."

"This is where everything is kept. There's nothing more we can do."

"But there has to be," I say, tears running down my cheeks. "There has to be."

Another silence envelops us. Calin's still holding me, I realise. The other two are standing by the archway, their heads bowed. No one is looking at me for guidance anymore. I have none. I've nothing to offer, except the only thing I have left.

I swallow back the tears, swiping at my cheeks with the backs of my hands.

"Okay," I say, looking at Vasara. "We've been down here long enough. We don't know if Rhett is still managing to keep Polidori occupied. You must get out of here with the books, now. What else do you need to break the spell?"

"You mean besides the sacrifice?"

"You have that. It will be me. What else?"

Vasara's eyes widen, almost bulging.

"Narissa—"

"Don't! There's nothing more to say. This is it. Either

one of us dies or all three of us are trapped here for Polidori to find, in which case we're all dead, the witches back at the chateau won't get their grimoires, and Rey won't get her life back. This is not up for discussion."

"It has to be."

"No, it doesn't. You haven't survived this long on sentiment, Vasara. This is the right thing to do, the only thing to do. So, tell me, what else do you need?"

She stares at me, eyes full of sympathy and her voice catches.

"I need salt to form the runes, but I have that. I brought some just in case."

"Okay, and what else?"

As she continues to scan down the page, Esther steps beside me. Her voice trembles.

"Naz, you can't do this."

"We don't have a choice."

"Yes, we do. We always have a choice."

"Not this time."

"Please let me do it. Let me be the sacrifice."

Tears prick my eyes. I could have guessed she'd say something like this. I may not have known Esther long, but over the last week or so, I've learned so much about her, like how deeply she cares and how much she will give to those she loves. It's the way of the wolves, I believe. A way I was just starting to understand.

"No," I say to her. "This is my mess."

"This is *our* mess. You're my Alpha. I'm your pack."

"And what a great job I've made of it."

"Naz, please. I know you don't see it, but you're the one

who brought us together again. You're the one who gave us a sense of hope again, a sense of purpose, after Juliette and your mother … after Ruth …" Her words drift off into nothing.

"You still have that," I say, taking her hand. "You do. I was never meant to lead. If Freya hadn't been my mother, you'd never have looked at me twice."

"That's not true. You have a power. A strength. Maybe it is to do with who your mother was, but does that really matter? People are born with some of the same talents and skills their parents have. That's nothing new. Naz, I can't let you do this. I can't."

I want to tell her the pack will be fine. Probably better than they were, without me there to screw everything up for them, but Esther has turned to the others.

"Vasara, Calin, please explain it to her. Tell her that it has to be me."

Her request is met with silence.

"They're not going to do that, Esther," I say.

I turn my gaze to where Vasara is pouring salt to form a series of symbols, matching those on the page next to her. There's already magic at play as the white grains turn black as they hit the ground, as if absorbing all the light that falls on them.

"I cannot decide for you," she says, "but the spell will be ready in a few minutes. I will light the candles, and when the time is right, I will need the sacrifice to step into the circle."

"How will I know when that is?" I ask.

"The flames will tell you."

"And all I have to do is step inside?"

"That's all you have to do."

This sounds like a simple way to die, preferable by far to death by psychotic vampire. I've faced worse possible endings in my time. Maybe now that it is inevitable, I'm actually going to get away with it easy.

"Will it hurt?" I ask. The question sounded so sensible in my head. A reasonable thing to want to know. But when the words leave my lips, they sound childish. Heat floods to my cheeks.

"I will do my best to minimise the pain," Vasara says softly, "but I can make no promises."

I nod. I have nothing more to ask her. My eyes turn to Calin.

"Can we?" I say, indicating further into the vault, wanting a moment's privacy.

He nods and we walk away.

37

It's darker back here than it was before. Vasara's light stays with her and the runes she is casting, but I'm grateful. Not being able to make Calin out clearly makes it feel like he can't see me either, even though it's not true, and with his vampire vision, he'll be all too aware of my tears. Still I'm grateful for the illusion the gloom provides. With a sniff, I wipe my cheeks, move towards him and rest my head against his chest.

The sound of my shallow breathing fills my ears as I wait for him to say something, to offer some words of comfort or reassurance or, better still, a way out of this. Maybe in the short time it's taken us to walk away, he's thought of something, another option that the rest of us hadn't considered. But after a moment of silence, the truth twists in my guts like a knife. There's nothing. This really is the end.

"I thought I'd have more time," I say to him as he runs his fingers through my hair. "I thought I'd get to grow old."

"I know," he says.

I think of when he faced his own mortality. Maybe he knows a little of what I'm going through. But it won't be the same. He still got to see his loved ones after he died. He still got to see the world, to travel, to exist. For me, this is it. This *is* the end. Or if it's not, I'm heading somewhere no one else has ever come back from before.

"Will you look after Rey for me?" I ask.

"Of course I will."

"If Vasara can't free her with the grimoires after all—"

"Don't worry. It will work."

"But if it doesn't. If she stays like she is, keep trying for her, please. There must be other spells in other books. Don't let that darkness win."

"I won't."

"And tell her … tell her I'm so sorry. Tell her I would have done anything I could to change what happened. Tell her I loved her."

"I will."

A torrent of tears is soaking his shirt. How do I tell him everything I need to, with so little time left? And my mind seems to have gone blank. I'm struggling to keep even a single thought straight in my head. The circle is all I can think about. Stepping into that circle. And then that's it. My life is over.

"And Oliver, too," I say. "Tell him I'm so sorry for how things turned out. Tell him I loved him. That he was always my best friend. That I never imagined we wouldn't have a chance to put things right."

"He'll know that."

"But you'll tell him? Promise me. And you'll have to convince him that it came from me, or he'll think you're just saying it to console him. You must make sure he understands."

"Of course I will."

And what about the others? I want Lou to know how much her friendship meant to me. How much light she brought to my life when my whole world had turned dark. And Chrissie, who was almost like a mother to me. And then Calin. What final words do I have for him? He's the only one I get to say goodbye to in person, and yet the words won't come.

"I wish I'd met you when we were both alive," I say, finally, at which he laughs.

"For that to have happened, I would have been immensely old, and I don't think you'd have found me half as attractive with no hair and saggy skin."

I try to laugh, but fail.

"You know what I mean."

"Yes, I do."

Pulling me closer to his chest, he plants a kiss on the top of my head and lets his lips linger there.

"You are a remarkable person, Narissa Knight. You're the most extraordinary thing to have happened to me in a hundred years."

Maybe there is something beyond this life. Maybe Freya and Dad will be waiting for me. I think of asking Calin whether he believes in anything beyond the here and now, when Vasara's voice calls to us.

"It's time."

The circle of salt is now bisected by a line, on each side of which a candle is burning. There are other symbols too, mostly between the circle and the archway. There are three stones with small tea-light-sized candles between them. I don't know what they're made of, but the smoke that weaves up from them is mauve and smells like earthy. If Vasara hasn't shielded the aroma, I can't imagine it will take the vampires long to smell something is up, which means we need to get moving.

"The first incantation will be to remove the spells currently working on us, the ones we share. Otherwise, when Narissa steps into the circle, we will all be affected," Vasara says. "From that moment, we need to move fast. Our scents will no longer be screened."

If there wasn't enough to worry about, they'll instantly become exposed.

"After that," Vasara continues, "I will start the incantation to break down the impediment holding us here. When the salt ignites, Narissa, you must step inside and there's no going back. Once you're there, you will not be able to leave and only when your life has ended, will the spell be broken."

Only when your life has ended. That's a slightly more subtle way of saying *only when you're dead*.

"I understand," I say. "We should get this started. We've already lost enough time."

"Okay. I won't be able to stop the chant. If I do, the barrier will likely draw power from me, rather than the other way around."

"And if that happens?"

"That's not something we have to worry about. Now, you have to step in by yourself and there will only be a limited window of opportunity."

"Right," I say. "I won't mess it up."

She nods, then kneels on the floor next to the open grimoire.

"Narissa?"

I hear the tone of Esther's voice and know what she's going to say again. I shake my head to silence her.

"Can you hold my hand?" I say. "Can both of you hold my hand until I have to step inside?"

"Of course," Calin responds. "We're here for you."

"Just don't let go until you have to, okay? Don't let go of me," I beg, not caring if I sound like a small child.

I suddenly realise what a luxury it is, having my two friends here supporting me. My father didn't get a last wish or any comfort in his final moments before Styx snapped his neck. Neither did my mother, shot without any idea of what was going to happen to her. I should be grateful for being able to prepare myself. And I want to be, but it's so hard.

I'm digging my fingers into their palms, my eyes closed, as Vasara begins to chant.

"*Sugriauti kliūtis. Aš išardau šią palatą.*"

"*Sugriauti kliūtis. Aš išardau šią palatą.*"

"*Sugriauti kliūtis. Aš išardau šią palatą.*"

The pages of the grimoire flutter, disturbed by a sudden breeze that sends Vasara's hair flying around her.

"*Jūsų jėga čia ne vanduo.*"

"I'm scared," I whisper.

"We're with you. You can do this," Calin says.

Esther doesn't speak, she merely grips my hand even tighter, so tight that I feel our pulses beating against each other. Sweat is making our palms slippery.

"Jūsų jėga čia ne vanduo."

"Jūsų jėga čia ne vanduo."

The salt circle erupts in flames. I'm startled. They're at least waist height, dancing and spitting in every shade of red and orange. The whole of the vault is aglow and our shadows flicker across the walls. The heat is so strong, I feel my cheeks burning. Every instinct tells me to back away. To get as far away as possible. But this is the moment Vasara told me I would know I had to go into the circle. I have to somehow make myself step through.

"Jūsų jėga čia ne vanduo!"

As Vasara continues her chanting, her eyes turn to me, and I can see the worry on her face. I know exactly what she's trying to communicate. I have to do it now, or it will be too late.

I close my eyes, allow myself one shuddering breath and drop Esther and Calin's hands.

38

It's now or never.

Battling every instinct, I move towards the flames. My skin is already scorching from the heat. Sweat is running down my forehead and spine. I'm so close, I can almost taste the burning wax. The earthy aroma, that before seemed so pleasant, is now suffocating. I quickly look back for one last glimpse of Calin and Esther, a reminder of who I'm doing this for. My eyes meet Calin's, but as I turn to Esther, she's gone.

She comes at me with such speed that I don't even notice her until her hands hit my chest, pushing me back towards Calin. I stumble and he catches me. A gasp escapes my lips as I realise what's happening.

"No!" I scream and try to reach for her, but Calin holds me tight as she steps through the flames.

"No!" I scream again and pull against his grip. "No, no, no!"

"It's too late," he says, still holding me fast, pinning my arms to my side.

Esther stands there, the bottom of her clothing turning every shade of orange and amber, but when she turns to face us, I see nothing but calm in her eyes.

"It's time for me to go and find Ruth," she says, her eyes shutting tight against the pain of the flames that are clawing at her, then dips her chin to her chest. Fire shoots upwards, as her clothes ignite around her, and then all at once, she's engulfed in a supernaturally bright flash.

"Let me go, let me go!"

I writhe in Calin's arms, but he holds me fast. I want to turn. I want to summon the wolf, but I can't. It's even more broken by what I've just witnessed than the human part is.

"It should have been me! It was meant to be me!"

"This was Esther's choice," he replies.

I continue to struggle against him, but I've little fight left. I'm defeated, and she can't leave the circle now, or we risk Vasara, too.

Amidst my screams, Esther falls noiselessly to her knees. A moment later, the flames extinguish of their own accord. Despite the inferno, her now naked body shows no evidence of the fire. If anything, she looks perfectly at peace.

"It's done," Vasara says, standing up.

Another seedling sprouts in her hand and she throws it through the archway. It lands on the other side, still perfectly green and intact.

"We need to go now. They likely heard you screaming if nothing else. We must hurry."

She bends to pick up her things which she hastily shoves into her bag, along with two of the grimoires. As Calin picks up his rucksack, I stay rooted to the spot.

"What about Esther?" I ask.

Vasara bites down on her lip.

"We could barely manage all these books when there were four of us, and this has drained me … we can't take her."

"No," I snap back, with venom in my voice. "We're not leaving her here."

"Narissa, I know you're hurting, but we have to be practical. If we don't get out of here, Esther will have given her life in vain."

"We're not leaving her," I say again, sobbing.

Calin is pulling on his grimoire-laden bag. I know he will do whatever I ask of him and beg him with my eyes.

"Fine, let's hurry though," he says.

Vasara and I hastily shoulder our packs, as Calin scoops Esther up in his arms.

39

Rhett

We hadn't set a time limit. As long as possible, was what I was supposed to give them. For as long as I could keep Polidori talking. But how long will be long enough? Calin said they'd be able to get down to the vault in a matter of minutes. Five perhaps. Ten if for some reason there was a delay. Then there'd be the same again for them to get back. But how long to find the grimoires? Five minutes? An hour?

Assuming all goes well, thirty minutes seems like a reasonable guestimate for them to be in and out again with the grimoires. More than half an hour has passed and I want out of this place, as soon as possible. But having Dimitar here complicates things, to say the least.

"So, what do I have to do to prove to you I'm on board with this *development*?" I ask.

"Development." Polidori rolls the word around his mouth. "Seems like an apt word. The newer vampires are calling it an uprising, but to be honest, we don't need to rise up. We're already far above the humans. We'll just be taking our rightful place at last."

"So," I say. "What do you need?"

Polidori takes a deep breath and pours himself a fresh drink. He's toying with me, which is completely fine. The longer he thinks he has the upper hand, the more he's helping me stall for time. I always thought this guy was arrogant, but he's taken it to a whole new level. I don't know why we were worried about him suspecting we were up to something. He's too conceited to see past his own ego.

Dimitar, on the other hand, is pacing the floor. As much as he agrees with Polidori's plans, he's a shallow creature who just wants the thrill of the hunt. Displays of intellectual power don't impress him. He's on board for the killing, pure and simple. The more he gets to do of that, the better. Some things never change. But if anyone's going to pick up there's something out of place here, it's going to be him.

"The region of Italy you live in," Polidori says, finally. "It's very quaint."

"I like to think so."

"And very ... human dominated, if I can put it that way?"

I don't like where this is going, but I haven't liked a single word that's left his mouth so far, so that shouldn't really surprise me. I play along with him.

"You've both been very gracious in that regard, giving me my space and seclusion," I say.

He laughs.

"You may be thinking a little too highly of us, in that respect," he says. "Rural Italy is not what it once was for us vampires, and why take a simple farmer, when you can have a Milan fashion model? Don't you agree?"

"I have always found country folk perfectly adequate, but I understand what you're saying."

"Well, what we need to do first of all, is to even up the numbers a little. And I have to say, having someone of your age and experience on side will certainly be to our advantage."

"Even up the numbers?" I query. My stomach, turns.

"Take as many as possible without drawing attention to ourselves. The last thing we want is the humans catching wind of us before we're sufficient in number to withstand any possible counterattack. Thankfully, we're nearly there in urban areas, but if we can assert our presence in more rural regions, that will eliminate a hiding place for them when we make our final move. You understand what I'm staying?"

"I believe I do."

In truth I know exactly what he's saying, and it makes me feel sick. This is the buy-in to prove my allegiance to him. Turn innocent humans to vampires. Something I have refused to do for four centuries, and I'm not about to do it now, either. I'm preparing to fake my best smile and assure him I will do exactly as he asks, when I catch her scent. It's subtle. The lightest of fragrances. She's hidden it under cloaking spells almost her entire life, but I'd recognise it anywhere. Vasara.

I watch as Dimitar's eyes narrow. He can smell it too.

"Polidori—" he starts, but I cut him off.

"How about we get those humans you offered me earlier back in here? Seal the deal with a drink?"

Polidori cocks his head to one side and looks at me inquisitively.

"I thought you weren't hungry."

"Sometimes it's not about the hunger, though, is it?"

His smile is unnerving, but it's what I need to see.

"Dimitar, if you would be so kind as to show our guests back in," he says.

Despite the order, he doesn't move. His brow is wrinkled. He's listening.

"Come on, Dimitar," I encourage, moving towards him and slapping him on the back. "What do you say? A drink to celebrate our new concord?"

Still, he doesn't move.

"Something's wrong," he says.

"Of course not. You should be pleased. Isn't this what you always wanted?"

Ignoring me, he moves towards the door.

"Ah, the famous manners I remember so well," I remark.

His head snaps back at me, his fangs exposed as he growls.

"Dimitar! That kind of impertinence will not be tolerated," Polidori says in a tone just short of censure.

But Dimitar's expression remains unchanged, his eyes still fixed on me.

"A witch," he says. "There's a witch in the building."

40

Narissa

I follow Calin up the stairs. We're moving fast but he's doing his best to carry her respectfully. I see her face as her head lolls back. Her skin has a luminosity to it in Vasara's supernatural light. Her lips are gently parted, as if she were simply sleeping. But she's not. She's dead. She sacrificed herself for me. And I will do this for her. I will give her the proper funeral she deserves.

"Keep going," Calin says. "We're nearly at the top."

I've just seen the first glimmer of light from under the door above us, when he stops suddenly and I bump into him.

"What are you doing?" I ask. "We need to keep moving."

"Quiet," he hisses back at me. "Something's wrong."

"Can you hear someone? Who is it?"

"I don't know."

I reach back for Vasara's hand. My heartbeat ticks out the seconds, louder and harder each time.

"Okay, let's go," he says.

"Is it safe?" I ask.

"It was never safe," he replies. "Just stay close and, Vasara, remember what I said."

"I know," she replies.

I look back at her, the obvious question there on my face.

"Now is not the time Narissa," she says.

I don't know what it is they've discussed beforehand, but if it prevents me getting Esther's body back for their funeral ceremony wolves need, I'm not interested. There's not a chance in hell that I am leaving this building without her.

Calin's steps are more tentative now, quiet and considered, and there's an unease radiating from him that I'm not used to. It's infectious. I can feel it spreading to Vasara behind me, too. She's muttering to herself. Maybe it's just an incantation to maintain the spell that's lessening the weight of the grimoires for us, but whatever it is, I'm feeling an impending sense of doom.

When we reach the top of the staircase, we step through the door that Vasara opened earlier with magic. After everything that's just gone down and with Calin's heightened anxiety, I was half expecting to be ambushed here. It's almost a surprise to find the corridor empty. The tension lessens a little. If anyone knew we were here, this would be the place to wait. The perfect place to block us off.

From here, there's only one corner to turn before we reach the vast entrance foyer that leads to the exit and the outside world. I offer a hesitant smile to Vasara, who does her best to reciprocate, but it doesn't reach her eyes.

"This way," Calin says. "You guys doing okay?"

Neither of us reply.

The weight of my backpack is increasing. I suspect Vasara's spell may be waning. I just hope it holds on a little longer.

I look at her again, trying to gauge if she's struggling and notice how tired she seems. Her skin has taken on a sallow, grey tone. Her cheeks have sunken inwards. When she said that the spell had taken a lot out of her, I didn't realise quite how much. As wrong as it sounds, Esther, in death, looks better than Vasara does right now.

"It won't be long," I say to her, reassuringly. "We're nearly there."

My voice comes out louder than the whisper I'd intended, and a chill of fear spreads through me. Could Polidori have heard that from where he is? I know Calin can hear conversations in other rooms, but I've never asked him how far that extends. I pick up the pace, helping Vasara as I go. I no longer care about the sound of my footsteps. I just want to get out of here, now.

We turn the corner as one and then freeze as one, too.

The volume of my voice would have made no difference at all. There was no need to worry whether Polidori could have heard me from the Council rooms. He wasn't there. He's standing in front of us, blocking our way to the door that separates us from freedom.

"Well, isn't this a nice surprise?" he says, with a grin.

41

A vampire, a witch and a werewolf walk into ... Turns out it's not a joke after all.

Polidori is not alone. On each side of him stands another vampire and both have their fangs out. One is Rhett and I don't recognise the other. He's stockily built, with cropped black hair. I don't know how I can tell, but he's old, too. Old and powerful.

"Calin, my dear boy," Polidori says with a long sigh. "This is so disappointing. I'd heard rumours, but I didn't want to believe them. The wolf girl? Really? And after she murdered one of our own?"

"Narissa is innocent. She killed Styx in self-defence. She didn't even know she was a werewolf until he scratched her and triggered her first transformation."

Polidori, turns his attention to me.

"So, you didn't set out to kill him. Is that the case, Miss Knight?"

"He killed my father," I spit.

"Yes, yes he did. A most unfortunate incident. I quite liked Michael, but he simply got too nosy. When he discovered the sleeper cells we were creating, I really was left with very little choice."

I feel my temper getting away from me. I slip the backpack from my shoulders and prepare to turn.

"Narissa, stop," Calin says.

"Why? We can take him now and end it. It's four against two, after all. Isn't that right, Rhett?"

In a flash, he has his arm locked around the other vampire's neck.

"I knew we couldn't trust you, you damned wolf lover," the vampire hisses at him.

"Perhaps you should have been ready for me then, Dimitar," Rhett replies.

Polidori turns to them with a hollow laugh.

"Dearest Rhett, I've been ready for you since the moment you arrived," he says and claps his hands together.

The front door swings open, and a stream of vampires flood into the lobby. There must be at least two dozen of them, and some are armed with more than just fangs.

Rhett reluctantly releases Dimitar, who pushes him towards us.

"Wait, Sir," Calin says. "We don't want to fight."

"Is that right? Then what explains all the vampires that have been killed across Europe? The broken nests that reek of her werewolf stench? I suppose that's nothing to do with you."

"Fine. Do what you want with me. Just let these two go."

"Calin you can't—"

"Narissa, this isn't a debate!" he interrupts, without even looking at me. "Please, I'll stay. Release them."

The corners of Polidori's lips rise in a smile, exposing the tips of his fangs.

"But I'm not interested in you. I'm disappointed in your behaviour, but I'll get over that the moment I've ripped out your heart. What I want right now is her."

He extends a finger in my direction and locks eyes with me.

"And what do we have here?" he asks, switching his gaze to Vasara. "A witch? How interesting. You know, I've recently lost possession of two of mine. You don't know anything about that, do you?"

Vasara stays silent.

"What about you, Narissa? I believe you were fairly well acquainted with one of them, the one whose body we still haven't recovered. Can you enlighten me?"

"Go to hell."

"Not a very imaginative response."

He turns back to Vasara.

"What do you say? Why waste your time stealing a few tatty little books like those?"

He indicates the grimoires spilling out of my backpack.

"I can show you where we keep the really good stuff. Think of what you could do with all that power at your disposal. Young Rey saw the possibilities. I promise you won't be disappointed."

Vasara presses her lips together and glances at Calin.

"Not yet," he says to her. "Polidori, let us pass and no-one needs to get hurt."

"You know that's not going to happen. And you know you don't have a chance, don't you?"

He turns back to me.

"You might be more than a match for these young vampires, wolf girl, but we ancients are made of sterner stuff."

I've seen Rhett in action, and I know he's right. I'm not so sure I could take Polidori, and even if I could, with all the others here, I don't see any way out for us. But I'm not about to back down now.

"You'll see what I'm capable of, soon enough," I say, hoping the fear I'm feeling isn't obvious, although it's clear from his smirk that it probably is.

"Tough talking, but I'd take a moment to think carefully about what you do next. I mean, you've lost one of your little troupe already, haven't you? A dog I presume?"

His face turns down in mock sadness.

The growl that escapes my throat is far more like a wolf than I would have liked.

"How sad for you," he chuckles. "Not that it would have helped you in the grand scheme of things. It still wouldn't have been an even fight, would it? You should have already worked out that you're not leaving here alive, let alone with even a single page from one of those grimoires."

"Let me do it."

It's the vampire Rhett call Dimitar who spoke.

"I'll kill them all for you and show Calin the true meaning of the word loyalty before he dies."

"How dare you question my honour?" Calin says, stepping forwards. "I'm the one who still believes in the Blood Pact. In peace."

He turns to Polidori.

"A way of life that *you* pioneered, that *you* made me believe in."

For a moment, Polidori's expression softens by a fraction, and his smile could almost be one of fatherly pride, if it wasn't for the fangs on display.

"My son," he says gently. "You do know that you have been that to me, don't you? A son, who I raised in my own home."

Calin says nothing.

"I always worried that your idealism would be your undoing. Yet I really did love you for it. It's why I turned you in the first place. How ironic that it's now the reason I'm going to have to kill you."

He steps forwards, fangs out and glistening.

Calin gently places Esther's body on the ground.

"Vasara, now!" he yells.

At this, she drops her pack from her shoulder, throws her head back and begins an incantation.

The screams that shoot through the air are bloodcurdling. They're so resonant that the cast-iron chandeliers hanging above us rumble. Polidori and the others have fallen to the floor and are clutching their heads, eyes shut tightly against what must obviously be an agonizing pain.

Whatever she's doing, I just hope she can hold it long enough for us to get the hell out of here.

I turn to Calin, ready to race away but see, in horror, that he's in exactly the same state as the others. His knuckles are white as he digs his fingernails into his scalp, and there's blood dripping from his bottom lip, where his fangs have pierced the skin.

I turn back towards Polidori and his army. Now is my chance to end it all, to take them out while their defences are down.

"Narissa, stop!" Vasara yells.

I can barely hear her, but the urgency in her voice makes me pause.

"You must listen to me. We need to get the grimoires out of here. I can't hold them like this for long."

"But Calin?"

"Calin is not our priority right now."

"I'll turn. I can kill them all."

"No." Vasara steps in front of me. "They're all connected. You kill one and you will kill them all, including Rhett and Calin."

I move to Calin and bend down next to him.

"Calin! Calin, can you hear me? Please, listen. You're going to be okay. You're going to be okay."

I can see that my words aren't reaching him. His hands have left his head, and his fingers are scraping at the floor tiles. The screeching sound they're making sends shudders down my spine. His nails are bleeding around the quicks. I snap up to standing.

CHAPTER 41

"What have you done to him?" I spit at Vasara. "Let him go!"

"I'm sorry," she says.

She's holding her arms out in front of her, palms up. There's a slight glow emanating from them that ebbs and flows like a pulse.

"It was our only choice."

"You have to let him go."

"It doesn't work like that. Do you think I want to see Rhett in agony like this?"

I shake my head, trying to steady my thoughts despite all the noise, but it's not working. The screaming is growing louder, and my inner wolf is now fighting me, wanting to take over and attack.

Polidori is doubled over in pain. Like Calin, his long nails are scoring the slate tiles. Right now, he doesn't look like a vicious killer, an immortal monster capable of ending a life in a heartbeat. But then I probably don't look like the Alpha wolf I've been masquerading as, either.

"Narissa, we have to go!" Vasara shouts at me.

She shoves a backpack into my arms. It seems to weigh more than ever. Picking up her own, she mutters something and the weight eases slightly.

"Come," she says and heads for the door.

I stoop and run my hand over Esther's body, then look back to Vasara. She shakes her head, before turning her gaze on Rhett. His skin has become translucent, his eyes are bulging from his head, but that's nothing compared to Calin. He's crumpled on the floor, his arms wrapped around his head again as he writhes in pain.

"Please, he can't handle this."

"This was the backup plan. He knew this could happen."

"What do you mean?" I say, but she isn't interested in answering any more questions.

"The spell won't hold forever," she says. "Please, Narissa. We have to get the grimoires out of here. We must go."

I freeze. We're down to two people now. The weakest two. And with Vasara needing to maintain her spell, it's up to me to do the carrying. There's no way I can take Esther, too.

"The grimoires!" Vasara yells. "Quickly, move!"

I force myself to stand and somehow manage to hoist a backpack onto each shoulder, trying to block my mind to Calin's wails and Esther's dead body. I'm almost choking on my tears and my vision is blurred. I don't want to leave either of them. I glance back one last time, and at that very moment, Calin looks up

"I'll come back for you," I whisper.

EPILOGUE

We step out onto the street and the sudden return to everyday normality shocks me out of my stupor for a brief moment. Vasara's hands are still moving, as she maintains the spell. Then we're bundling into the back of a black cab for the short journey to our own car.

The next thing I'm aware of, Vasara is leaning across me from the driver's seat and fastens my seatbelt. Where are we going? Then I remember. Dover. Now she's chanting once more, presumably setting a spell to ensure we're not followed.

Then there's silence.

As she drives, one thought keeps going around in my mind, on a loop. There were five of us when we started out on this, and now there are only two. One of my pack is dead, abandoned, and we've left Calin and Rhett behind, too. What will Polidori do to them for their betrayal? Death seems too easy an option.

Only when the car rumbles up the ramp onto the ferry, do I start to become more aware of my surroundings.

Vasara finally speaks.

"Calin knew the risks," she says. "It was a fail-safe to get you, me, Esther and the grimoires out, if things went south. It was our Plan B."

"Then why didn't I know about it? You should have told me."

"You would have tried to stop us. Like you'd have tried to stop Esther if you'd known she was going to take your place as the sacrifice."

"She told you?"

"Not explicitly. But I thought it was a strong possibility. As, I'm sure, did Calin."

So, I'm the only one who couldn't sense what a member of my pack was thinking. What a fabulous bloody Alpha that makes me.

"They'll be killed, won't they?" I say. "Polidori and that other vampire, Dimitar, they'll kill Calin and Rhett."

"Not straight away, I don't think."

She looks ahead, focusing out beyond the windscreen, despite the fact we've parked up.

"They'll want to make them suffer, first."

"Oh great."

My voice is dripping with sarcasm, but when she turns to me, there's a softness in her look.

"It's actually a good thing. Polidori wanting to exact revenge like that means he will have to keep them alive. Which also means we'll have the chance to rescue them."

Maybe, a few days ago, I would have been up for the challenge, but I've already lost so much.

"I'm not sure what a few witches and a few dozen wolves can achieve against a vampire army."

She tilts her head.

"I think you're forgetting a couple of things."

"Like what."

"First of all, we have those." She indicates the bags containing the grimoires on the back seat. "And I'm about to use them to free the most powerful witch I've ever met."

I have to concede she has a point, but even if Rey is everything she believes, I'm still not convinced it will be enough.

"And second?" I ask.

She smiles.

"You're an alpha, Narissa. It's time we summoned the rest of your pack."

Can Narissa rescue Calin and stop Polidori? Find out now in Dark Reckoning, the final book in the Dark Creatures Saga!

SCAN ME

Just how old is Rhett and what is his connection with the first of the werewolves? Claim your collection of FOUR prequel novellas and discover the secret of Rhett's dark past. PLUS, get information on new releases and exclusive content.

NOTE FROM ELLA

First off, thank you for taking the time to read **Dark Redemption**, Book 4 in the Dark Creatures Saga. If you enjoyed the book, I'd love for you to let your friends know so they can also experience this action-packed adventure. I have enabled the lending feature where possible, so it is easy to share with a friend.

If you leave a review **Dark Redemption** on Amazon, Goodreads, Bookbub, or even your own blog or social media, I would love to read it. You can email me the link at ella@ellastoneauthor.com

Don't forget, you can stay up-to-date on upcoming releases and sales by joining my newsletter, following my social media pages or visiting my website
www.ellastoneauthor.com

ACKNOWLEDGMENTS

First off thank you to Christian for his amazing covers for the whole series and Carol for her diligent editing.

To Lucy, Kath and all the alpha and beta readers who have helped shape this novel, I'd be lost without you.

And lastly, thank you to all of you readers out there for taking a chance on my book. I hope it has bought you as much joy reading it as it did for me writing it.

Printed in Great Britain
by Amazon